Spinifex: The Curse of the Night Parrot

Spinifex:
The Curse of the Night Parrot

John Grant

Stormbird Press

Stormbird Press

Stormbird Press is an imprint of Wild Migration Limited.
PO Box 73, Parndana, South Australia.
www.stormbirdpress.com

Cover night parrot illustration by John Grant,
also printed on page 231.
Taxonomic illustration, by Elizabeth Gould (1804–1841)
Cover design by Stormbird Press.
Typeset by Alice Teasdale, Big Quince Print.
with Antique Olive and Kazimir.

National Library of Australia and State Library of South Australia
Legal Deposit
Grant, John, 1959 – Author
Spinifex: The Curse of the Night Parrot
ISBN – 9781925856439 (hbk)
ISBN – 9781925856422 (pbk)
ISBN – 9781925856446 (ebk)

*The publishing industry pulps millions of books every year when
new titles fail to meet inflated sales projections—ploys designed to
saturate the market, crowding out other books.*

*This unacceptable practice creates tragic levels of waste. Paper
degrading in landfill releases methane—a greenhouse gas emission
23 times more potent than carbon dioxide.*

*Stormbird Press prints our books 'on demand', and from sustainable
forestry sources, to conserve Earth's precious, finite resources.*

We believe every printed book should find a home.

This book is dedicated to those who protect the spinifex country, its creatures, and its people.

Cultural Acknowledgement

This book was written mainly on the traditional land of the Mullunbarra-Yidinji people. We acknowledge the true owners of these lands—lands that were never ceded, sold, or given up. We pay respect to First Nations Elders everywhere—past, present, and future—and stand in solidarity with all First Nations people.

A Message From the Publisher

Literature has shaped the world, but it is the language of brave authors, like John Grant, that reveal truths and realities that are often difficult to communicate. There are grave responsibilities for activist authors when shining light into dark, hidden crevices. The writer must provide insight and guidance when interpreting his society, his world, but strenuously avoid perpetuating injustices of the past and present.

Wildlife crime is one of those dark, festering fractures we rarely talk about. It deserves illumination, but exposing it means carefully examining unconscious biases about race and identity. Grant has bravely explored the nuances of this contemporary tragedy in *Spinifex: The Curse of the Night Parrot*, giving form to a complex story that is impressively close to the real world.

Before I entered publishing, I worked on the front lines of the conservation movement in the international fight for the intrinsic rights of nature and connected communities. Wildlife crime was a major focus of this work. stood shoulder to shoulder with indigenous and local community land and environmental defenders from around the globe. My journey to that roll was, without question, easier and smoother than for many of my colleagues. My life struggles were nowhere near as profound, nor deep. But, in that space, I genuinely felt there was nothing that divided us. Together, we spoke a simple truth to power—humans are not separate from nature, and by devastating nature we are destroying ourselves. We were united in our condemnation of the colonial system, the great harm that lies at its feet, and the pain caused by its love-child, the privileged, modern western world. Spinifex echoes those voices.

At the beginning of the wildlife crime arc there are often indigenous and local communities who are closely involved, often fighting the crime and, more frequently than is comfortable, losing their lives. If you hold any doubt about that statement, I suggest you type 'land defenders' or 'Global Witness' into Google and follow any one of the hundreds of harrowing stories that will be revealed. Yes, there are exceptions, but even then the financial gains at the front end of wildlife crime are tiny. From the second step onwards the arc becomes uncomfortably, racially white or Asian and the profits gained immense.

When Grant created his characters in *Spinifex* it was important to him to give a sense of the imbalance of this crime. He could have restricted his characters to those who share his ethnic background, but to do so would have meant excluding indigenous characters from a novel set in the Australian outback, which not only rings as untrue, but is also disrespectful and disingenuous about where wildlife knowledge genuinely lies and who the true heroes of wildlife crime are. To avoid any risk of accidental cultural appropriation, he has created a fictitious community identity.

The book industry is increasingly closed to white authors writing about other ethnicities, without them first demonstrating thoughtful and important reasons.

I agree with this self-conscious stance. We need to build a publishing world that is genuinely inclusive of everyone. Yet some stories are important to tell from certain vantage points. Doing so illuminates the truth of what is happening. Wildlife crime needs to be called out with an honest voice. Grant is bravely forging this ground.

Dr Margi Prideaux
Publisher
December 8, 2021

Elizabeth Gould (1804–1841)

Chapter 1

Butler tensed as the familiar trio walked into the departure lounge. Looking away as casually as he could, he collected himself while tracking them from the corner of his eye.

As they passed, he observed that the three men were uncharacteristically quiet. Simo, the oldest of them at sixty-ish, was habitually loud and dominant but now seemed subdued. He walked with an overly casual air, faintly bandy-legged too, and wearing trainers instead of his usual natty ankle boots. The youngest one, Nonoy, disguised his gait a little better, but his fidgeting betrayed his edginess. All three wore loose-fitting long pants which flopped untidily over their shoes. As they sat, they kept their feet planted stiffly on the ground. They had timed their arrival carefully. The flight to Manila was called shortly after they sat down.

Butler's tipoff had come from a source in the local aviculture scene. His mole had always proved reliable and four weeks of close surveillance had given tantalising clues he was right again; nothing concrete, but enough to keep the investigation simmering.

Pepe, the middle one, grew restless as the other passengers formed a queue. He surely knew there was little chance they would be intercepted once they left Cairns; the rabbit warren of Manila airport was easily threaded by those with connections.

Customs wouldn't interview the three smugglers unless Butler asked, and he had no intention of doing that. He wanted all three men safely on that plane so they could be tracked at the other end. He had surprised even his maverick side with this latest tack, but considered his actions justified because his boss at Parks continually frustrated his legitimate efforts.

His biggest concern was the doped birds undoubtedly hidden beneath those baggy trousers. He had seen far too many beautiful, innocent creatures wasted.

As the line shortened, Pepe began to furiously tap his foot while he glared out of the grimy window. Simo quietly mouthed some reassurance. Nonoy, who casually glanced past Butler, reeled in shock. His eyes grew whiter and his hands clenched as he whispered urgently to the others. Butler stood calmly and stretched as he half-turned to see what the fuss was about. The federal police uniform of Gordon Prescott was coming towards him. What the hell was he doing here?

Butler hastily rearranged the startled expression on his face as he walked straight towards Prescott. "Keep walking," he hissed as he came within range.

Prescott clumsily half-stopped. Butler tried to cover the bumble by stepping off-balance as if they had almost collided.

Prescott strode away while Butler headed down the corridor to the toilets. As he stepped through the door, his phone signalled an incoming text.

PRESCOTT: What's happening?

Butler wanted Prescott gone. His first thought was to text *No Show*, but the clown was likely to come and talk to him. Besides, that didn't seem plausible given his terseness outside. He wasn't sure how convincing his sidestep had looked or how carefully the nervous trio had been watching him. He texted back, Stay out of sight!

Walking back into the boarding lounge, Butler glanced down at his phone while trying to catch the trio in his peripheral vision. He sensed them watching him. Swivelling his phone subtly, he took a photo in their direction. When he zoomed in, three pairs of eyes were glued to him.

Come on boys ... stay calm ... stay calm.

With only one other flight leaving from the far end of the terminal, Butler knew he would stick out even more if he didn't join the shrinking line for Manila. It felt like a game of cat and mouse as he joined the end of the queue, trying to come up with a plan.

He was known to the security staff but not holding a boarding pass was bound to attract attention. The suspects watched his every move as they stubbornly remained seated. Explaining this scenario to Prescott would be no picnic either—the cop was probably watching him on CCTV right now.

The brittle air felt as if it could snap. Butler turned his back on the three men, hoping to send the right message, but reflected in the inky lounge windows their silhouettes stayed put. The final call for the flight came through; still they sat. Six places to go until Butler reached the gate. Fear swelled in his chest.

Come on. Now! He willed them to join the queue. They sat.

Three places to go. His increasing anxiety hammered home how much he was putting on the line here. He pressed a ringtone on his phone, stepping from the queue to answer. He kept his back to the chairs.

Bloody Hell!

Prescott strode towards him, a look of disbelief and annoyance plastered across his face.

Butler turned to see Pepe leap to his feet and sprint-walk towards the toilets with Nonoy on his heels. Simo headed for the far end of the lounge.

"Get the old guy!" Butler barked at Prescott as chaos broke free.

By the time Butler reached the corridor, all three suspects had started running. The door to the men's toilet slammed open, then the women's. With a sinking heart, he realised they had split up. He charged at the first door almost bowling over a shrieking woman who hurried out. He yelled an apology as he leaped for the top of a locked cubicle. Pepe, pants and tights around his ankles, held a sleepy parrot in each hand. "They are my pets; I've had them for years ...", he whimpered.

Butler would have laughed at this brazen bluff if he wasn't so riled. He swung his arm down and unlocked the stall from the inside, barging through the open door.

"Hand them over!"

Pepe glanced into the toilet. Butler raised a fist. He hadn't punched anyone since high school, but he was in too much of a hurry to take no for an answer.

"Don't make me hit you, mate."

Pepe slumped against the wall, his eyes wet and beaten. Butler snatched the two gang-gangs, their tails cut to stubs. He ran out the door.

"Hang on to those, and that one in the ladies' room," he blurted as he thrust the birds into the arms of a security man.

In the men's toilet, a sickening flush raised Butler's blood to the boil. He kicked in the cubicle door, dived past a half-sprawled Nonoy and plunged his hands into the toilet bowl. An object brushed his right hand, but he came out with only two long blue feathers. He shoved his left hand in as far as he could but found nothing. He slumped back on the floor, kneecapped by how agonisingly close he had been. He squeezed his eyes shut, his groan erupting into a low growl. If there was one thing that could move Butler's thoughts to violence it was senseless cruelty to animals.

He glared at Nonoy who was pinned in the corner in his underwear. The poor bastard was petrified, his eyes moonlike with fear. Butler's wrath collapsed on itself.

"Get your pants on, mate."

After a long night of interviews, Butler found Prescott waiting for him.

"Job done, Butler, but what on earth were you waiting for in there?"

Butler's calculated deception in that morning's meeting had backfired, and now he was ill-prepared to explain his actions. He had downplayed the case, convincing Prescott he had had nothing to go on.

Prescott wasn't letting go. "You've got some explaining to do. You could have picked them up anytime, with my help or airport security."

Butler's muscles tensed. It was Prescott's arrival that tipped the smugglers off.

"I wasn't satisfied they were packing anything," he lied, "and I didn't want to scare them off for nothing. They might have used another airport next time."

"So much for you Parks blokes being good at spotting that stuff," Prescott countered.

"Yeah, well maybe I'm slipping." Butler gritted his teeth and took a deep breath. "Anyway, thanks for your help, Gordon, but listen, please let me know next time you're going to appear on an op like that. You took me by surprise and I wasn't sure how to handle it."

"Yeah, sorry mate. But next time give me the heads-up. I didn't expect to walk into that kind of action."

"No, it's not what any of us expect," said Butler. "Well, it's been a long night Gordon, no doubt we'll catch up over the paperwork."

"Yeah, see you, Ric. Have a good night."

Butler hurried away, wondering if his explanation of the night's events sounded plausible. He could only hope so.

Butler flopped on his bed. The mouthful of cold beer he gulped helped him to push aside his discomfort. Picking up the phone, he hoped for a decent connection to Manila.

"Ric, how are you mate?"

Considering his line of work and the constant clicks and whirrs on the line, Boy Reyes' familiar voice sounded almost annoyingly upbeat.

"Hi, Boy. Wish I had better news."

"What happened, Ric? We're waiting on that flight."

"I was so sure I could see them safely out but they were picked up. Nothing I could do about it. I'm sorry, Boy."

"It happens, Ric. Have they leaked any information?"

"They claim to be acting independently, just out for some easy money."

"Loyal smugglers, eh?"

"More scared than anything. Anyway, they'll be out of the game for a while now."

"Hmm ... they'll be relieved to stay in custody if the reports about their *kumander* are true. Word is something big is about to happen in Australia so I'm suspecting they've let him down at a bad time."

"Anything concrete?"

"No. But I will let you know what I hear."

"Okay, Boy. Sorry again about tonight."

"We'll find the big man soon enough. Maybe next time."

Butler's functional black bedside clock read 12:00 midnight. Behind it stood an old photo of his mother.

He felt the familiar ache of having known her so briefly and so poorly. Her olive skin and piercing brown eyes hinted at the Mediterranean. Beyond that and his father's sole contribution of a surname common enough to be untraceable, he knew nothing of his heritage—except that it mattered more than it used to. Tonight, with the two drowned parrots in his thoughts, his rootlessness pierced like a thorn.

Chapter 2

Butler had anticipated the weekend with special pleasure. His best and oldest friend was getting into town for another of his fleeting visits. A senior academic at their old alma mater and the academic high-flyer that Butler once wanted to be, Bob Harrison now ran a research program on the Cape York Peninsula, radio-tracking his beloved palm cockatoos from a little Cessna he had learned to fly in double-quick time. Adding string after string to his formidable bow, Bob landed fat research grants, collaborated with the luminaries of international ornithology, made the cover of 'Science' magazine, and still found time to be a devoted husband and father. He was the kind of industrious overachiever Butler lazily resented. Yet for Bob all Butler felt was affection.

The two had met as postgraduate students, each full of promise in their own way. On shared field trips they discovered—in the diffident way of young men—that they were both incurably romantic. "I'm going to ask Juliet to marry me," Bob announced into his beer over a twilight campfire one night.

"Geez, mate," said Butler, "next thing you'll be having kids and there'll be hell to pay."

"I hadn't thought of that," laughed Bob, confident his high school sweetheart would accept his proposal and that they would live happily ever after. "What about you and Ginni? Are you going to make an honest woman of her, or what?"

Butler gave a knowing grin.

Within a year they were both married; a year later both separated. Their friendship had intensified as they rebounded from crushed young love, driving out to the Victorian Mallee to clear their heads under the river red gums.

"Do you think she's out there, Ric?" asked Bob, staring up at the Southern Cross through the flimsy canopy.

"You mean, the One?"

"Yeah. Hey, what if there is only one and we both fall in love with her?"

"Give me a break. She'd pick you anyway. You're better looking. And you'll have a PhD."

"So will you."

Butler grimaced in the dark. "I don't know, Bob ..." he said, confessing to his nagging doubts for the first time. "I'm not sure whether I'll stay the course. I'm tired of the academic life already and I'm only beginning. I look at those jaded old lecturers of ours and I don't think I can stomach it as a career. I look at the undergrads we tutor, the good ones, and I see that excitement in their eyes, like I used to have."

"You could master all that stuff. It's just a matter of slogging away at it, that's all. I can help you." Bob's concerned face showed his distress at the thought of their lives diverging.

"Maybe I could, Bob, but it's just not me. I'm not into that stuff the way you are. I don't know what I would do, but I'll always want to work with wildlife, no matter what."

Having Bob visit him in Cairns always brought up that old question in Butler's mind. What if he had finished his PhD? He knew he would never have become the consummate academic that Bob had; he loved fieldwork, but he had no fondness for the tools of the scientist's trade—statistics, lab work or esoteric conceptual analysis. Over the years, he entertained the idea of getting back into the world of research, maybe writing up some pet projects he had tinkered with, but he admitted recently it was probably never going to happen.

As the years passed, Butler's doubts about his choices had been eclipsed by the certainty of Bob's friendship. It was that rarest of intimacies that could pick up where it had left off a year previously, a grounding influence in both lives.

Bob was sitting outside their favourite coffee shop under the flame trees. He looked up from the weekend papers, his face cracking into a familiar grin. Butler walked into his outstretched arms feeling the sorely missed pleasure of their embrace. Both men shammed a manly hug for the benefit of onlookers.

"You old bugger," said Butler as he sat. "When are you going to start looking your age?"

"You're not looking so bad yourself, mate. The public service must be treating you well."

"I wish," said Butler. He thought about how much of a bad mood he could fall into if he spoke about work. "It's frustrating, as usual ... I mean the fauna squad as it stood is long gone, and there's so few of us now who even care. And get this, they've handed most of the wildlife matters to the flippin' RSPCA who have got even less funding than we have." Realising he had said too much, Butler sighed. "Enough about that; I need a coffee. And tell me about your trip, mate. How are the cockies?"

Bob shook his head, swivelling the newspaper towards Butler. "I take it you haven't seen this."

"I don't read Rupert's bullshit anymore——" began Butler, but he had already spotted a most remarkable picture. The photograph was obscured by watermarks of the paper's logo, but the fragments showing through added up to an image that surely couldn't be what he thought. "No way ..." he muttered. He glanced at Bob who was clearly savouring his reaction.

A dumpy, speckled-green bird; its yellow belly, barred tail, fine legs, and a parrot bill visible in fragments.

"Where the bloody hell did this come from?"

"Have a read." Bob signalled to the waiter.

Butler's eyes sped across the page, stopping before the end of the first paragraph.

"You've got to be joking! Jim Elder photographed

a bloody ... It can't be! It is. It's a friggin' night parrot! It's got to be. I'd heard the rumours, but with him you never know."

Butler scanned the rest of the article while an amused Bob looked on. After every few lines he peered harder at the photograph, trying to pinpoint any clue it might be a fake.

"Could it be a ground parrot, Ric? A young one?"

"Not a chance. Look at that belly. Besides, the markings are all wrong and it's too squat. And look at the spinifex in the background. It's the wrong country for a ground parrot."

"Given Elder's past form, everyone will be suspicious."

"You can say that again, but honestly it looks as though he's got the goods this time."

"We'll find out during the show-and-tell he's planning to give in Brisbane. I'd love to go, but I've got a hell of a lot to catch up on when I get home and a conference the day after his talk. I doubt I'll make it."

Butler sat back, taking a sip of coffee. This was an exciting story but a wrench at the same time. For decades, he had nurtured plans of going out to spinifex country to search for the night parrot.

It had been more than a hundred years since the last specimen was shot; the bird feared extinct until 1990 when a roadkill showed up in South West Queensland. A freak of chance had left its corpse to dry out on the lonely roadside, in exactly the spot where his friends Walter and Wayne from the Australian Museum had stopped to take a leak. The remains of another night parrot, this time decapitated by a fence, were found 16 years later in the same region but, apart from a handful of claimed sightings, the bodies were the only evidence the bird still existed. Butler, like most avid birders, had always been fascinated by the night parrot. But unlike most, he kept a special notebook where he collected old records, notes on habitat, rumours—anything that might lead him to the mythical bird. With several places in mind for expeditions and a few tenuous connections that might have helped drum up funding for the search, he had longed to be the first to photograph the bird.

"Looks like he beat you to it, mate." Bob could read him like an open, large-print book.

"Yeah ..." Butler pushed aside his swelling disappointment. "Still, what's he going to do with this discovery? Someone with research experience needs to follow up, find out exactly what's going on with these birds. Elder is a great naturalist, but he has no formal training."

Bob frowned. "I don't fancy our chances of getting anywhere near it. He can't abide scientists; the cocky bastard was staggering under the weight of that chip on his shoulder last time we saw him. You watch, he'll be keeping this close to his chest, waiting for a chance to make money out of it."

"Is it money he wants or the kudos of being named the ultimate naturalist?"

"He might have just achieved that," said Bob, pointing at the newspaper. "Maybe I'm being too cynical, but once a collector always a collector, and birds are a meal ticket for him. I'm not saying it's wrong to make a living from wildlife——"

"But endangered species are on the wrong side of the line," added Butler.

"I don't disagree for a moment, mate." Bob clinked his cup off Butler's. "Elder can't be trusted. Not for a second. Don't forget Iron Range."

Almost a decade had passed, but Butler hadn't forgotten Bob's climbing lines being mysteriously cut. The fishing lines which acted as rope leaders for the subsequent climb of cockatoo nest trees had been slashed; by someone familiar with the nests' locations. Rumour pinned Elder as the culprit after he was overheard complaining to his tour clientele that the lines were endangering the birds; another example of academic ignorance. Bob was especially incensed since he always paid meticulous attention to the safety of the birds. Any tree where he couldn't operate in complete confidence, with the lines secured well out of the birds' possible flight paths, was excluded from his study.

A few months later, when Elder returned to Iron Range, Bob confronted him. It was pure coincidence Butler chose that day to visit.

Marching into his campsite, they were surprised to find Elder drinking beers with a group of rough looking strangers, his chalky face flushed red from the day. Where was his tour group? Elder introduced the men as birdwatchers from Sydney, but it was obvious to Butler the loud, profane drunkards were nothing of the sort. They hadn't batted an eyelid when a manucode called right next to the camp. Fortunately, Bob had had the good sense to know that evening wasn't the time or the place to confront Elder.

The following morning Butler accompanied Bob on his rounds of the nest trees. A two-week-old egg in the first nest had disappeared. A goanna or python were the most likely culprits. "All part of the ecosystem," said Bob, but the discovery did nothing to quell his broodiness.

At the second tree, a newly hatched chick nestled in its woodchip-lined hollow. After recording some details, Bob descended with a proud fatherly grin. "Little beauty," he purred, showing Butler a photo. But no sooner had Bob reached the next nest when a hail of expletives rained down. He rappelled down at speed, burning his hand. "Somebody's taken the egg and I can hear the bastards. They're at the nest up on the ridge. Let's go!" he hissed.

"Bob, hang on! Are you sure that's a good idea? We don't want to get into a fight with those mongrels."

"Yes, we bloody do!" There was no stopping Bob in this mood. "I've got a flare gun and an axe handle. They're not getting away with this!"

They ran towards the ridge with their meagre arsenal, the shrieks of a panicked palm cockatoo ringing loudly ahead of them. Bob's adrenaline got the better of him and their approach was anything but quiet. By the time they got to the tree the thieves had gone, a still-swinging rope dangling from the hollow. Bob was panicked. "We have to get to the other trees before they clean them out!"

Butler grew jittery. He dreaded tangling with

smugglers in the bush, no matter who they were, but he'd back Bob or go down swinging.

The next nest was a two-kilometre drive. Bob led a mad dash through the scrub back to his truck. They were almost there when they heard another vehicle's spinning tyres. They surged onto the road to find Elder standing by their ute. He raised an arm as they stopped in their tracks. He had a machete in one hand and a small cardboard box in the other. "They've gone, the arseholes," he shouted. "They heard you coming. Didn't want to take on the three of us. Shit, I'm glad to see you. They could have beaten me to a pulp."

"What the hell just happened?" demanded Bob, stalking up to Elder with ill-concealed rage.

Elder spoke calmly. "It's my fault. I showed them some of these nests yesterday. Then this morning, they broke camp early to go birding. I smelled a rat so followed them and parked in the scrub further back. When they got back to their car with this box, I bailed them up. The eggs are in it."

"Shit! I've got to get them back to the nests," cried Bob, torn between relief and panic.

"How did you get four burly blokes to hand over that box?" asked Butler.

Elder raised the machete. "They weren't armed, not even a brush hook, and I had this. It was enough to make them think twice. But they would have had me if you hadn't arrived."

Bob exploded. "You're a lying bastard, Elder! There's no way they gave you that box."

"Calm down, mate," said Elder. "You think you're

upset. How do you think I feel? I could have ended up in a shallow grave. Do you know how much these things are worth?"

"No, but I bet you bloody do! Put the box down, Elder!" Bob was swinging his axe handle menacingly now. "You better get the hell out of here before I put you in a fucking grave, you bloody thief! First you cut my lines, now this. I'm going to make sure you're hauled over the coals for this!"

Elder placed the box carefully on the ground, then pointed the tip of his machete at Bob. "Listen, mate," he spat, "you're upset, okay? I understand that. But I've saved these eggs and probably a few more besides. And yes, I cut some of your lines. I found a dead eclectus parrot under one of those trees and it seemed you weren't being careful enough. You bloody academics are all the same, no friggin' idea about the real world, no common sense. All you're interested in is keeping yourself in a cushy bloody job. I know more about birds in my little finger than you'll ever friggin' know! And do I get any credit for it? Of course not. I don't have any letters after my name! You're all pathetic, the lot of you."

Bob clenched his fists and stared at the ground.

"You'd better go," said Butler.

Elder glared at him, slowly backed off, and disappeared through the trees.

Even with Butler's eyewitness testimony and Bob's detailed notes, nothing was ever pinned on Elder. Avoiding Bob since then, Elder evidently didn't read the publications coming from the research at Iron

Range. If he had, he would have known that eclectus parrots lying dead under nest trees is a regular event; casualties of the warfare between females for scarce hollows.

The palm cockatoo eggs had been returned to the nests that morning and both survived to fledging, but they forever remained a distinguished duo. Along with all the other chicks tagged in the project, their genetic signature had been taken from a blood sample, but by the time the lab results came in it was too late to switch them. They were the only ones raised by foster-parents.

After breakfast at the flame trees café, Bob and Butler adjourned to a bar for a quiet beer and a few games of pool—a tradition started in postgraduate days. Their conversation turned to family, friends, and holidays. For a short while, Butler forgot about drowned parrots and faded ambitions.

It wasn't until he drove Bob to the airport that their conversation turned to women. "I hate to ask, Ric, but you haven't mentioned Melissa. Are you two okay?"

Butler sighed as he thought about his girlfriend of the past two years. "Yeah, she asked after you, too. Ah look, she's a lovely woman. Well, I don't have to tell you that, but I just don't know if she's ... you know ... she can tell that I'm not sure, but what I haven't said to her is that I'm not sure I can ... really love her anymore."

"Is it because of what happened between her and Aramis?"

"No. I mean, we moved on from that. Besides, I don't think they ever ... I don't know. It's so hard to put a finger on it, but I just feel numb sometimes, like I can't move beyond a certain level. We were going fine and then from out of nowhere came this pressure, as if she needed proof I was committed to her. She wants to get married."

"Do you?"

"Y... eeaah ... I guess so. Although I didn't say it like that to her. I said yes. One day. She can tell I'm hesitating, but I don't know why. Maybe I'm not certain I want to be with her for the rest of my life. Am I making sense?"

"No," said Bob, trying to keep a straight face but failing. "Sorry, mate, beer talking. Listen, I can relate. That's how it was with me and Sal for a while. I didn't get it either, still don't, but we both agreed to stick with it. I'm glad I stuck it out. It strengthened our relationship."

"Thanks for the advice, Dr Bob. Have I told you you're a goody two-shoes?"

Bob gave Butler another bear hug at the airport. "Give me a ring if you need to talk. And don't let Elder get you down. Sorry he beat you to the night parrot, but he'll get his just deserts one day. Maybe sooner than he thinks."

"Why's that, mate?"

"The curse," whispered Bob, narrowing his eyes for dramatic effect. "Shane Parker saw a night parrot in the 70s and died before he could publish his sightings. Old Fred Andrews collected most of the known specimens in the 1800s and drowned in a foot of water, in the middle of a bloody desert."

The hairs rose on the back of Butler's neck. "You're not usually one for superstition, Bob."

"No, but you are." Bob guffawed and slapped Butler playfully on the shoulder. "I bet you've got the chills already."

Chapter 3

Monday morning brought Butler heavily back to earth. Planning to slip quietly past his work's reception desk, he found his way barred by the behemoth backside of his boss. Weagle turned, curling his lip as he caught sight of Butler.

"Don't go anywhere, Butler. I want to see you in my office in five."

His cold grey eyes betrayed a malice Butler expected of such a summons. Weagle resumed his conversation with Melissa, whom he liked to treat as his private secretary, mainly so he could leer down at her from his intimidating vantage point. She caught Butler's eye as he shuffled past, her knotted eyebrows hinting she hoped to talk with him soon too. Her expression reminded him he had failed to return her calls again that weekend. He flinched at the reckoning he couldn't put off much longer. The reception desk was no place to discuss personal matters, but perhaps they could meet after work. If he could just get through today, maybe tomorrow he would have a better idea how to broach that conversation.

As on most mornings—but especially Mondays—Butler sat at his desk and considered tendering his resignation. The meeting with Weagle would be a follow-on from Friday's briefing, when he had tried to marshal the hydra, the multi-headed taskforce charged with controlling wildlife smuggling in North Queensland. As senior field officer for the lead agency on this case, it fell to Butler to assemble his counterparts from Customs, Quarantine and the Australian Federal Police whenever there were developments. Friday's briefing had been a predictably frustrating half hour, but he had won a small victory. His presentation ensured no other agencies would assist him at the airport the night the smugglers made their run. Why Prescott had barged in, he still wasn't sure.

"Hey, *Harry?*" Weagle's lieutenant and errand boy Tom Houlihan poked his head around the corner, addressing Butler from an ever-expanding double chin.

"Karl will see you now."

Houlihan, an ex-cop like Weagle, was as corpulent as his boss but nowhere near as venomous. Butler mentally scratched his head for the umpteenth time, wondering why on earth this twosome had ever joined the Queensland Parks and Wildlife Service.

He knew better than to hope the weekend had softened the bollocking he was about to get. Weagle's moods were volcanic, a longer build-up inevitably leading to a louder bang. As Butler approached Weagle's door, he heard him bantering jovially with someone.

From the tone, and the visitor's suit and close-cropped hair, he was a cop.

"In you go," said Houlihan. "I'll wait here; I don't want to miss this." A fleck of jam on his lip betrayed his early start on the smoko donuts.

A vein bulged from Weagle's forehead when he sighted Butler. "Detective Bill Smallis, this is Ric Butler, senior field officer and senior birdbrain. No offence, Butler."

Let me count the ways, Karl. Butler smiled weakly.

"Hang on," said Smallis, "You said his name is Harry."

"Just our little joke," laughed Weagle. "Harry Butler is obviously our boy's hero and role model."

Smallis sniggered childishly and shook Butler's hand.

"Look, Ricky, I'll get straight to the point and offer some constructive criticism. You need a hand with things; intelligence-gathering for example. The surveillance data you presented was ... well, to call a spade a spade ... inadequate. I know you boys are understaffed and underfunded, but you can't carry on as if you're detectives. Eh?"

Butler stared at him dumbly. "Help is always welcome, Detective."

"Damn right. If you had got these guys on infrared video, say, you might have gathered real evidence. Give us that kind of information and we can get a warrant, search their premises and pick them up. Easy."

A flash of annoyance washed over Butler, but he forced his mouth to remain shut.

Smallis was on a roll. "Seeing cardboard boxes delivered at night and bulk birdseed being bought doesn't cut it. It's circumstantial at best. Eh? Look, you got lucky on Friday night, eh? But if Gordon hadn't gone in there, you might have blown that chance."

Butler met Smallis' interrogation-room stare with his best dumb look.

"Karl, keep a better eye on this one," said Smallis. "We're supposed to be working together, eh? Without better intel I can't supply AFP officers. None of us have the resources to go off on these wild-goose chases. We're hard-pressed chasing real criminals——"

"You mean a wild-parrot chase, Bill," laughed Weagle. He sneered at Butler. "Polly want a cracker?"

Butler's knuckles whitened as he squeezed the edge of his chair.

Smallis' shoulders rocked with unsuppressed mirth.

"Seriously," he added, "ask if you need advice about surveillance gear. Eh?" Glancing at his watch, he stood and flicked Weagle a wink as he shook hands. "Gotta get going, Karl. Good to meet you, Harry. Sorry, Rich, wasn't it?"

Butler wasn't getting a parting handshake. "Yeah. Thanks for your advice." He got up to follow Smallis out the door.

"Hang on, Butler."

Weagle waited until the door closed behind Smallis before the smile drained from his face. "Do you see what an embarrassment you are, Butler?"

Butler thought it best to assume the question was rhetorical.

"Your ineptitude has made this entire department look bad. Friday's briefing was a bloody joke and you know it. Through dumb luck you managed to collar some amateurs but not without making us the laughingstock of Cairns." He slammed shut a desk drawer. "And as for the way you handled things at the airport ... You go off half-cocked like that again, you'll face the consequences."

"But they were smuggling——" began Butler.

"And don't you dare ask Smallis for help," snarled Weagle. "I'd have to do some serious arse-licking before they'd even consider it." The eruption intensified. "I'm sick of you thinking you're the only one who can save the planet from the baddies. What a fucking joke! It's insubordination, Butler, and you're full of it. I tell you who to investigate and when."

"But he offered to——"

"Shut it, Butler! I won't have innocent people targeted by you, on the say-so of some dodgy tip-off. If you don't cut the crap, you'll be cleaning dunnies out in Winton. Understand?"

Butler bit down hard on his lower lip, then nodded. "Sorry, Karl."

"Now piss off out of here."

Butler marched back to his desk, his gloom lightening as he thought of Elder's show-and-tell in Brisbane. It would attract a who's who of Australian parrot enthusiasts and researchers. Perhaps one of them would have heard whispers about upcoming smuggling activity.

"Ric, can we talk?"

He spun around. "Can we do this later, Meliss? It's not a great time."

She sat down and folded her arms. "There's not going to be a good time, is there?"

Butler felt trapped but could tell she wasn't going anywhere. "Sorry, I meant to call you yesterday."

Melissa closed her eyes and took a deep breath.

"Honestly, Meliss. I've been preoccupied."

"Tell me about it. But it's not just that. You've been drifting away from me for months and I need to know what's on your mind."

Butler's mind froze. He knew the pain etched on her face was all his doing. The honourable thing to do would be to ease her suffering by telling her the truth.

"I'm sorry, Meliss. I ..." He struggled to know where to begin, even after multiple rehearsals of this scene.

"This isn't working for you, Ric. I don't know why, and I feel like you'll never tell me. But I *need* to talk through the hard stuff."

She was right. He never really let her in. What caused him to hide behind his work, he didn't know.

"I care about you a lot, Ric, but I can't go on like this. We had some good times, and you're a lovely guy ... but unless things change ..." She wiped her eyes and stood up. "See you round, Ric."

Butler's head dropped. "Perfect," he muttered.

Chapter 4

Butler made it from Brisbane airport just in time to slip into the room as the M.C. finished his introduction. "And now, ladies and gentlemen, the man you have all come to hear, our modern-day adventurer, Mr Jim Elder."

Elder basked in the adulation of the applauding crowd, his rugged physique appearing uncomfortable in formal attire. Under the cover of the ovation, Butler headed for an empty seat at the back of the room. He registered a faint twitch of Elder's heavy moustache as the bushman's taut gaze stalked him across the room.

Composing himself, Elder began. "You know what I have to show you today, but I hope I can still surprise you." Despite his heroic status, he spoke with a self-consciousness that betrayed his nerves. "When I finally photographed the night parrot for the first time, it was like a dream." He warmed to his part as encouraging murmurs rose from the audience. "But it took a lot of hard work."

Elder's story was one of relentless pursuit,

painting a picture of long days of driving, endless nights of listening, and monotonous months and years of fruitless effort. Following the slenderest of clues with a doggedness verging on mania, his tenacity had finally achieved the impossible.

Butler scanned the awestruck faces of the naturalists, academics, and public servants in the room. As he picked out several old acquaintances and a few friends, he made mental appointments for after the event. A collective intake of breath refocused his attention on the dais. Elder theatrically raised the projector's remote and pressed the button. A stunned silence greeted the first slide. Any doubts that had lingered in the room melted away. The image was clear and detailed, the wraith become flesh. Every vibrant green feather was sharply focused, the larger ones encrypted by dark markings, growing finer on each smaller covert, subtler still on the mantle and the cowl, finally dissolving on the head into a web-like tracery broken only by the eye. Butler peered into that dark eye, stung by an aching for that small creature.

Butler's head seemed to swell, his temples throbbing as his visceral reaction caught him off guard. The surrounding room silenced, and the crowd faded into blackness. A faceless fear that raised the hairs on his nape blunted the excitement of seeing this myth made real, and a vague panic squirmed up towards his throat. He coughed, gasping as if he had stopped breathing for a moment. He sheepishly looked around, thankful the crowd remained entranced by the picture. Elder's voice droned in the distance. The next picture came up, but Butler heard little of what was said until the slideshow was over.

The floor was thrown open for questions. The first one, from the well-known birding guide Chuck Crawford, was predictable. "Will a recording of the call be made available to researchers to search for the bird?"

"No way," smirked Elder. "It's not in the night parrot's interests to have people swarming around in its habitat."

Crawford's voice raised. "The location needs to be revealed to state agencies for the protection of the parrot."

Elder suppressed a chuckle. "It is my opinion this very sensitive species needs to be left alone. I will personally work with the landowner to protect the bird from threats, especially cats, and keep the property's location hidden from overeager twitchers and photographers."

A murmur of discontent rippled around the room. Sandy Harrington, a senior figure at Birdlife Australia raised her hand. "Jim, you must appreciate the urgency of knowing more about the distribution and ecology of the night parrot." The murmur grew progressively louder. "For all we know you could have found the last one in existence. To protect the species, we need to conduct surveys in suitable habitat, and a recording of the call is a vital tool in facilitating those surveys."

Elder nodded as if he was actually considering the statement. "My priority is to protect the birds I know about right now. I will do more surveys using private funding and those people I think are committed to the best interests of the bird. I won't be releasing a recording of the call."

Sandy's face mottled crimson. "If that call is not made available, significant night parrot habitat could be lost to mining developments, inappropriate land management ..." She trailed off.

Heads nodded but an unmistakable note of dissent also swirled about the room. Without waiting to be called upon, Graham Cooper, the eminent and passionate ornithologist, leapt to his feet and pointed at Elder. "Do you expect us to leave the fate of this bird in your hands? It's not your property we're talking about. It's a priceless part of our heritage, a ... a national asset, a critically endangered species. It concerns us all, not just you. The proper authorities need to manage it." Cooper's voice faltered.

The MC stood nervously and approached the microphone, but Elder motioned calmly to him to sit down. Carefully spoken, and without drama, Elder's words had an air of finality to them, showing nothing or nobody would change his mind. "Well, my opinion of the *proper* authorities, as you call them, is well known. Their half-arsed attempts at managing our heritage caused the night parrot to be endangered in the first place." His voice rose another notch and his face flushed. "And why haven't the *proper* authorities found them before now? Because they haven't bothered looking! Privately funded conservation is achieving more than any state agency, and that's the track I'm heading down."

Bickering broke out across the crowd as advocates

of the night parrot defended their positions. Across a swirl of waving arms and reddening faces, Butler watched the bushman's expression. A grim satisfaction crept under Elder's imperious moustache. As he gathered his things from the podium, his eyes met Butler's. He seemed on the verge of recognising Butler's face when the MC interrupted. Butler was certain Elder had not yet placed him.

"Ladies and gentlemen. Ladies and gentlemen! Please." The MC shouted into the microphone. "Thank you for your obvious interest in this evening's talk. Clearly this topic warrants further discussion, but the media have been waiting patiently so we must adjourn. But first, please thank our man of the hour—a living national treasure, Mr Jim Elder."

Despite obvious opposition, Elder received a flood of applause worthy of any State of Origin match. Steve Borrow, whom Butler hadn't previously noticed among the gathering, leapt to his feet. Sensing Butler's gaze, Borrow turned and met his old colleague's eye. As he was swallowed up by a standing ovation, Borrow flushed red; because of an old or a new unease, Butler couldn't tell.

"How about a beer, mate?" Butler turned to find Bob grinning at him. "Bit noisy in here."

"I didn't think you could make it," said Butler as they headed for the door. "It's great to see you."

"Miss this? I mean it is kind of historic, never mind the national treasure bit," laughed Bob. "I'm not sure if Elder was planning on the reaction he got."

"I don't know. He seemed to enjoy it," said Butler

as he took a seat at the venue's bar. "He didn't mind stoking the fire either."

"I didn't think you'd be here to see it either, mate. Cheers."

"Weagle ticked me off so much, I chucked a sickie. He exploded when I requested time off to attend Elder's little shindig. He even told me to stay away from Elder, threatening me with——"

"Ric! I thought that was you, sneaking in late." The voice boomed from behind.

"Well, if it isn't Mr. Big himself," chuckled Bob.

"Ah, the two musketeers. How are you, Bob?"

Brett Venables, an old friend from the Cape and a gentle giant of a man, shook hands warmly with each of them, his meaty paws enveloping theirs.

"I'll have one of those, innkeeper." He pointed to Bob's beer and winked at the barman. "A toast to our newest national treasure." His eyes twinkled mischievously as he glanced over his shoulder. "Was that over the top or what? I'm glad I didn't come here to learn about the night parrot. Instead, I'm an expert on Jim Elder's monumental achievements."

The three clinked glasses, then retreated to a quiet spot as the crowd swarmed around the bar, hotspots of debate still flaring.

"He's determined to keep this to himself," said Brett. "Obviously doesn't want government involved. Do you reckon he can evade the system like that?"

"Yeah, it's an interesting one," said Butler. "He may need permits at some point, unless he just tries to fly under the radar. If he can raise the funds he needs, he can do whatever he wants mostly. Especially since we don't know where to find him or the birds."

"He will need a lot of money to do anything significant, protection-wise," said Bob. "Just getting the feral cats under control will cost a small fortune."

"Well," whispered Brett, glancing around, "rumour has it he is bankrolled by foreign backers. European, I understood. Take that how you will, but he may have generous funding now he has succeeded."

"Any suspicious backers?" asked Bob. "Might be mates of yours, eh Brett?" he teased.

Brett narrowed his eyes, mock-threateningly. "Hmm ... that's still a sore point. My case is still active, but the corrupt buggers won't let me see my file, no matter how much I wave FOI at them."

"I can't work out what Weagle is playing at," said Butler. "To accuse someone of fauna smuggling, with no evidence, and then to leak it to the papers. Who knows what goes on in his mind?"

"Someone's got it in for me," mused Brett. "Anyway, how about another beer?"

"I hate to run out on you fellas," said Bob, "but I must love you and leave you. I'm off to Perth in the morning."

"Great to see you, Bob." Brett reached for Bob's hand. "Give me a ring next time you're up north."

"Will do, Brett. Ric, can you walk with me?"

Bob placed his arm around Butler's shoulders. "Are you okay, Ric? You seem a little flat."

"You know me too well, mate." Butler heaved a sigh, grateful for the chance to talk openly. "Meliss spoke to me after Weagle's tirade and caught me hopelessly unprepared. She was really upset and suggested I ... well, she said a lot of things but told me she needed more. I don't know if she'll ever speak to me again."

"Are you going to try to make things right with her?"

Butler sighed again. "I don't know, mate. There are too many other things on my mind. Look, I know you're in a hurry. I'll call you when you get back."

"Do that, Ric. I'm glad you told me." His phone rang. "It's Sally. Sorry, mate. Call me on Wednesday."

Butler lingered outside under a sunset chorus of noisy miners until a cool subtropical breeze drove him back inside. Brett and Steve Borrow were in deep discussion. Both looked like headlight-stunned rabbits when they spotted him walking towards them. He tried to catch Borrow's eye to greet him, but Borrow quickly shook Brett's hand, gave a brief wave to Butler, and left.

"I don't think Aramis knows whether you've forgiven him, Ric."

"I don't know either, Brett."

"Tell you what though, he's in with the man of the hour. He's the only scientist the treasure will spare more than two words for. Looks like he'll be the research brains on the team."

"That should be interesting," said Butler, arching an eyebrow.

Chapter 5

It was still early when Butler pulled up at the service station in Mount Surprise. The main and only street of the gem fossickers' haven was quiet apart from the bickering of apostle birds. A flight of pink and grey galahs divided a glorious blue sky as they rocketed in over the power lines. They landed in a flurry, as if snagged on the wires, and launched into a cacophony of shrieks and squabbles. Butler smiled. The dry country birds always gladdened him, especially the loud larrikins and their sun-catching colours. He breathed a contented sigh, deciding the trip had already been worthwhile.

Opening the door into the cave-like shop roused a haze of dust that danced and swirled in the single sunbeam penetrating the room. Through the murk, brain-like haematites, staring agates and exploding tourmalines gleamed from rusted skeletons of shelving. Fossils of fish, plants and ammonoids glowered from the opposite wall.

"You vant somesing?" came a stern voice from

behind a large trilobite on the shadowy counter at the back of the shop. A skull-like object was just visible behind the fossil, its dull onyx eyes berating him. Wisps of dust-coloured hair completed the likeness of a Bornean dried head.

The skull blinked. "Can I help you?" it spat.

"Sorry to disturb you ..." began Butler.

"You ain't disturbing me, it's a shop. You vant to buy somesing?"

"I'm looking for directions, if you can help. I'm trying to find Jim Elder."

"Ach! Ze bird man. Anuzzer reporter, hoh?" queried the skull.

Butler accepted the shop owner's deduction rather than disclose his own purpose, if he even had one. The ghoul grew impatient.

"Go towards Georgetown, take ze last driveway on ze left, about two kilometres from here. His name is on ze gate. You buying petrol or vat?"

Out of courtesy, Butler bought twenty dollars' worth. As he headed west, he marvelled at how backwaters like Mount Surprise acted as magnets for misfits and crackpots. It was another of his favourite things about being out west. A place he might fit in himself, one day.

He found the driveway easily, realising Elder's earlier directions, or lack of them, had been a ploy to discourage him. The rutted track was about a kilometre long, and Butler could see why it was the naturalist's choice for a bush retreat. Wallabies crouched between tufts of grass, two emus sprinted across the track, and squatter pigeons played Russian roulette with the car at every twist in the road. A shadow darkened the car as a flock of black cockatoos drifted overhead. As he forded a shallow stream, a low mudbrick structure with solar panels obscuring most of the northern roof came into view. "My kind of place," thought Butler out loud as he coasted into the yard and parked beside a well-worn truck.

Elder marched around the house with one finger raised in front of his lips. A flicker of recognition crossed his face.

"I'm filming out the back," he said in a low voice. "Follow me."

Butler followed the stocky figure into the backyard. Elder's thick forearms swung loosely at his sides, his greying hair squashed under a khaki hat, military style like the rest of his clothing. He motioned to a pair of deckchairs on the shady veranda, taking the larger one and again pressing his finger to his mouth. "Sit a few minutes," he whispered.

An expensive-looking video camera mounted on a heavy tripod faced a small pool. The surrounding sand, rubble, and withered grass provided the bush birdbath with a natural backdrop. Within the branches of some nearby shrubs, small birds flitted anxiously. The first to appear was a humbug-like double-barred finch. Two more followed, drinking nervously before darting back to cover. Another bird of similar shape flitted to the pool. The sun illuminated a heart-stopping palette of blue, yellow, green, and deep lavender. Butler gasped in wonder. It was the first wild Gouldian finch he had ever seen. Elder caught his eye and nodded. A smile played over Elder's lips as three more Gouldian flew in to drink, their black heads bobbing as they eyed the deckchairs.

"It's not much," said Elder, "but I call it home. I've spent ten years burning, seeding, slashing, and watering just to get these Gouldian here. They'll nest in about a month."

Butler's attention riveted on the finches, but, as Elder prognosticated, he heard a subtle change in the bushman's voice. Elder enjoyed being challenged.

"How do you know they'll nest?"

Elder feigned surprise.

"When you've seen as many Gouldian as I have, you can hear their testes growing." With a cocked eyebrow he stared at Butler.

Butler didn't know whether to be impressed or confused. "How did you work out how to attract them, Jim?"

"Pay attention to what you see. Not too many people know how to do that anymore. A dying art, I suppose."

"Is that how you found the night parrot?"

Elder's green eyes narrowed. He swivelled towards Butler. "Good things come to those who wait."

The quenched finches disappeared into the long grass. Elder walked to the camera and checked the display.

"You were in Brisbane. You heard how much time and effort I put into that bird. Nobody else could have done it. I found the night parrot because I thought like a night parrot. I became one."

Elder's voice took on an evangelistic tone, his eyes vacant as he stared past Butler.

Butler shifted uneasily in his seat. The slight movement shook Elder out of his trance. His brow knotted. "Ric, right? What did you want to talk to me about?"

Butler sensed Elder's patience ebbing.

"Well, Jim, you're the only person who can help me. You've spent a lot of time in the Southwest, and you're obviously tuned into what's going on out there. I'm wondering if you've spotted any suspicious characters—trappers, that sort of thing."

"Yeah, I've seen them, and damn me if I can't stand them. Stealing our wildlife and for what? A few lousy dollars. The worst ones are those arseholes with a foot in both camps, like Silva. Or that Brit ... what was his name?"

"Gardiner?"

"That's him. Posed as a respectable aviculturist, treasurer of the national society for crying out loud, then bought illegal birds behind everyone's back." Elder's eyes grew wider. "And robbed his bank customers to finance it. You couldn't invent a story like that."

"Silva maintains he was framed, you know."

"Of course he does. Pull the other one, it's got bells on it."

"So, Jim, about the night parrot. I think you're doing the right thing keeping it to yourself. The fewer people know about its location the better, as long as——"

"You're damn right!" Elder bellowed. "Who would I

tell? Those dickheads at bloody Parks? Useless bunch of pricks. They'd stuff it up like every other bloody thing they get their hands on. Birdwatchers? Don't make me laugh! Bloody twitchers don't give a shit about the birds. They're as bad as any other collectors. Scientists? Hah! They're so far up themselves, they're biting off their own noses!"

Elder's skin turned livid red around his cheekbones. The conversation was derailing, and Butler's careful toadying was going to waste.

"So, Jim," interjected Butler, in as soothing a tone as he could muster, "Have you heard of anybody operating in Western Queensland?"

"They're all over the bloody place. Who's to stop them—Customs, the police, Parks? None of them are doing a damn thing and they're rotten all the way to the top. No one can stop them."

"What do you mean 'all the way to the top'?" Butler was keen to keep that runaway train rolling but was met with a stony silence.

Elder's tone became less persuasive.

"I rave on sometimes."

"It's okay, Jim, really. I hate the bastards too. That's why I stay in this job. I'm trying to help."

Elder looked at the ground and nodded.

"Sorry I can't be more help, but like I told you on the phone, I have to collect my wife from Cairns airport this afternoon."

As they walked to Butler's car, Elder caught his eye. "I've met you before, haven't I? I thought I knew you in Brisbane."

Not wanting to dredge up Iron Range, Butler

harked back to his university days when he first met Elder through a fellow student. "Years ago, Jim. I was with Andy Tallon a couple of times when he visited you."

"Ah! The Goshawk-man. What's he doing now?"

"I lost touch. Last I heard he was chasing harpy eagles in Mexico."

"That's right," Elder laughed. "He did a Jimmy Buffett, didn't he? Got a Mexican cutie and not a tattooed one either. So that was it, eh? That was a while ago."

Butler started the car engine.

"Listen, mate," said Elder. "Don't mention the finches to anyone."

"You have my word." He shook hands with Elder through the open window.

"I don't want those academics out here bleeding the poor little things. Useless pricks."

Butler was in no hurry to return to Cairns. He bought a sandwich in Mount Surprise, opting for the second service station, and drove to a small dam he had discovered years previously. Under the shade of wild plums, he settled on a comfortable flat rock to eat his lunch. Elder's words buzzed around in his skull, but he couldn't decipher them yet. Breathing in, he smelled eucalypts mixed with the tang of the fine mud exposed along the bank. His head cleared as he soaked in the solitude. He closed his eyes and drifted off to earlier bush days.

His mother's voice wafted from another waterhole

he had all but forgotten. A salty lagoon in the flat country, with skies that stretched forever. He was a small boy seeing his first ever jet-trail. His mother told him there were people sitting in that shining speck, flying off to somewhere. He had planted his bare feet into the red earth, fearful for anyone so far up.

"What if they fall?" he asked, grabbing his mother's arm. She pulled him closer.

"They won't fall, baby. They're flying to a big city like Brisbane. Or Cairns. I visited Cairns once. Not by plane mind, but I will one day, and I'll take you with me, Riccy." She tickled him under his chin. "Maybe they're going to Hong Kong!" she giggled. "Maybe you can take me there, Riccy, one day when you're grown up and have a job."

He had never given her that plane trip. After she died, he moved to Cairns first chance he got, and he'd been there ever since.

Regret nibbled at him as intensely as the heat from the flat black stone. Emotionally drained from recent events, he gratefully soaked in the calm of the bush. He woke under a heavy sun falling to the west. His uneaten sandwich crawled with ants. He sat bolt upright, startling a handful of leaves from the trees. In his sleepy stupor, he imagined bright green leaves swirling over the dam, rising, then reattaching to the twigs. The insistent chittering of budgerigars rang around the gums until in a heartbeat they were off, racing in a pack between the branches. He couldn't remember the last time he had seen such a flock. He sighed, not wanting to leave. He left the sandwich to the ants.

By the time Butler reached Ravenshoe, his stomach was rumbling and his head swam with thoughts. Something about Elder didn't sit right. His passion appeared genuine, but he had never properly answered Butler's question. He seemed intent on deflecting it, and yet, it was a simple question: had he run up against any wildlife traffickers in the field? Unless the answer was too difficult. Elder's sheepishness at the end of their conversation didn't add up. "I'm not much of a detective," Butler quietly reprimanded himself, wondering whether he'd been lied to, laughed at, or both.

He stopped at the top pub, 'Queensland's Highest,' for a counter meal. Ravenshoe was quiet on a Sunday evening; its pleasant country town feel a world apart from Cairns, only a ninety minutes' drive away. The barman set him up with a welcome beer while he waited for his meal. Elder's words gnawed into his thoughts. He knew plenty about the wildlife trade. It seemed unlikely he didn't know who was operating locally, but he wasn't giving anything away. Yet his concern for the birds was touchingly real.

Butler's dinner was surprisingly good, warranting two glasses of red wine. As he ordered the second, he committed to staying the night. He followed the wine with a double Drambuie before booking into his room. He stumbled on the stairs, realising he had had more to drink than usual. But it had been a queer day. He had relished parts of it; the freedom he felt in the bush, and the birds. The whirling budgerigars, his mother's favourite, had lifted his spirits to a high seldom felt of late.

Maybe I'll quit this bloody job. He sobered under the hot shower. Go off on a road trip, camping and birdwatching every day. God, I love it out here.

He fell, half dry, onto the bed, his head spinning from alcohol and dreams of liberation. Yeah, that's what I'll do. I'm no good at this job anyway. Someone else can do it. I'm going bush to find a night parrot of my own.

Chapter 6

The dam at Mount Surprise formed a distant memory by the time Butler was out west again. On his own terms this time. He dozed in the warm winter sunshine in the little park on the outskirts of Mount Isa. From the bench where he lay, spinifex-dotted hills surrounded him, echoing with the lunatic cries of friarbirds. His best and oldest friend Bob crouched in the shade nearby, boiling the billy. Bliss.

Butler stretched out, placing his hat on his face to keep the glare from his eyes; the narrow beams of sunlight forming patterns as they chinked in through the eyelets. Soon he snoozed peacefully.

Boom! A peal of distant thunder invaded his sleep. It seemed out of place in such a blue sky. Boom! again, closer and rumbling for longer, waking him. The third Boom! shook the bench. He pulled the hat off his face, trying to discern from where the noise was coming. He tried to sit up, but his body was sluggish. Twisting his head, he caught sight of an object moving slowly towards the park just as the next Boom! sounded. It was a night parrot. A twenty-foot-long night parrot, deep red all over. It raised one foot and stepped closer. Boom! In slow motion, it crashed its foot down shaking the earth violently beneath Butler. He fell from his bench as the parrot entered the park, staring vacantly at him. He couldn't get up. His phone started ringing. Boom! The parrot pursued him, its blank eyes menacing. His phone kept ringing. Where was Bob? He called out, but no sound came from his mouth. Boom! The red hills trembled. His phone rang, sounding louder ...

With a muffled cry, Butler woke in a completely dark room. His sweaty hair stuck to his forehead and his head thumped in protest at the ringing phone. The phone's light glowed under his clothes. He groaned as he rolled over to reach for the phone, falling awkwardly from the bed.

Damn. Ravenshoe. Weagle's name lit up the screen. Bugger ... what time is it?

"Yeah, Karl——" he rasped.

"Oh, Sleeping Beauty! Not disturbing you, am I, Butler?"

"What time is it, Karl?"

"I don't know what time zone you're in, Butler, but it's after eight o'clock here."

"Damn. Sorry, I'll be there soon."

"You'd better be. You haven't heard then?"

Chapter 7

Butler's aching head still reeled from Weagle's news. Elder had been found dead. How could he be? Just yesterday the guy was larger than life.

"Hey, Birdman!" Houlihan's voice echoed across the foyer of the Parks office.

Leaning out his office door with the phone trapped under his fat neck, Houlihan smirked. "How about your boyfriend, eh? Stupid ass got himself butchered. So much for fame and fortune, eh?"

Butler dragged his feet to Houlihan's door. "What have you heard?"

"Not much. Elder's wife found him dead last night. And get this. The police called Karl at the crack of dawn after discovering a Parks vehicle was there yesterday. He wasn't too happy when he worked out it was you. Naturally they want to talk to you, since you were the last to see him alive. Apart from the perpetrator, that is. Hey, sorry Harry, you don't suppose you're a suspect, do you?"

"Don't be silly, Tom," Butler parried, only now

realising he could indeed be a candidate.

Houlihan raised his eyebrows. "Yeah, right," he muttered sheepishly, then brightened. "Anyway, you'd better get down to the police station." He tilted his head towards Butler's desk and raised his voice a notch. "And you better take your new boyfriend with you."

Butler faced his desk, his eyes locking with those of a young black man who wore an Akubra.

"Who the hell is he?" said Butler, "And what's he doing in my chair?"

Houlihan sniggered. "Must be your present for being a good boy, Harry." He waved Butler off.

Weagle, who was talking on his phone, rapped on his office window to draw Butler's attention. He silently snarled and gestured in the newcomer's direction.

As Butler approached his desk, the young man stood and smiled. His lean frame, angular face, and dark, curly hair spoke of the inland. Butler introduced himself and shook the man's hand; the newcomer's eyes bored into his as if he recalled his face.

"Jake Varoy," he said, offering a limp handshake. "Your new offsider. What happened to the last one?" He grinned but his expression quickly changed to one of embarrassment. "Sorry, maybe I shouldn't have asked, what with——"

Butler stared at his feet. "Sorry, Jake, but I've never been a babysitter, and I don't need to start now."

"Way the boss explained it, I'm your backup."

Butler struggled to make sense of all that had happened in the last few hours. He was too tired and too choked to argue about it, and an over-shoulder glance at Weagle told him the boss was in no mood to entertain his objections.

"The police want to interview me; we'd better get over there."

Cruising into downtown Cairns, Butler felt the dark stare on his cheek. "Do I know you mate?" he snapped, regretting it instantly.

"Nup," came the calm reply.

"What's your story, kid, how come you got lumped with me?"

"I'm not too popular at the moment," breezed the youngster. "Got put where I won't do any harm I suppose."

Realising Jake might be a fellow maverick, Butler's scalp relaxed. The straight talk made a welcome change. He chuckled, his tender head reminding him last night's alcohol hadn't worn off just yet.

"So, what made you so unpop——"

Jake interrupted his question. "Where you from, Ric?"

"Grew up in Brisbane."

"Grew up there, eh? Born there?"

"No, out bush a bit from there."

"Like out west?"

"What is this, mate, the Spanish Inquisition?"

"Sorry, mate, just my way. You know, Murri way."

"No, I don't know," protested Butler.

"Just my way of getting to know you. Where you come from, who your mother was, your father, you know. Lot of Butlers out my way."

Butler took a deep breath and sighed it out.

"Listen, Jake, no disrespect, but I'm having a rough day. Maybe later, okay?"

"No worries, Ric. But can you bring me up to speed on what's happening? Please?"

Butler paused. "Fair enough ..." he said, "but pass me a couple of Panadol, would you?"

As Jake rifled through the glovebox, Butler pondered where to begin. "This guy, Elder, who's just been killed—I can't believe I was with him only yesterday—he found the long-lost night parrot." He glanced at Jake expecting a confused look.

"Yeah, saw it in the headlines. Go on."

"You saw the story then?"

"Yeah ... poor old parrot never knew it was lost."

"Hmmph ... yeah anyway, Elder has ... had ... a history. You probably read that too, but it goes deeper. Egg collecting and so on. But I ..." he hesitated.

"Yeah?" Something in Jake's voice and manner gave Butler the feeling he could be straight with him.

"Well look, I'm just working on my gut feelings here, but I know he's somehow connected to this big smuggling operation I've been working on. I'm not saying he's ... was ... bent, but he knew something. He was hiding something."

"You gotta watch those gut feelings, Ric. They can get you into trouble."

Butler sensed Jake spoke from bitter experience. "So, you were saying why you were so unpopular."

"No, I wasn't," Jake answered casually. "But since you asked, and you're my boss, sort of, it's only fair you know that people think I'm not too good at doing what

I'm told. That's just their opinion, mind. I try to do my job the best I can."

Butler pouted his approval. "Where have you been working up till now?"

"Western Queensland, mostly. But they wanted me out of there, so ... here I am. I think I got this job because they didn't know what else to do with me. I don't have any experience chasing after wildlife smugglers, but Weagle said you could use the help."

Even in his weary state, Butler felt confused that Weagle would offer him assistance. After weeks of solo surveillance, he wasn't about to argue but it didn't sit comfortably. Still, Jake was a breath of fresh air. "I think we'll get on fine, Jake."

Butler was escorted into an interview room where an efficient Senior Constable Eileen Petersen took a statement from him. Tall and nordic, with a sharpness of grooming that straddled the boundary of self-confidence, she wrote notes on his recorded account in a small, precise hand. Butler described his meeting with Elder in as much detail as he could, sticking to what he had seen and heard. Small details he had forgotten until now—subtle expressions that crossed Elder's face, a glimmer of melancholy in his posture—sieved through his mind as he focused on reconstructing the conversation. As he wound down his account, Petersen looked up at him coolly, her silver-blue eyes seeming to cut through him.

"So, you left Elder's house at 11 o'clock yesterday morning. That makes you the last known person to have seen him. Did he mention his plans for the rest of the day?"

"Yes. He was about to drive to Cairns to pick up his wife at the airport. She'd been away. That's why he had only a short time to talk to me."

"Did he seem anxious, disturbed ... anything on his mind, maybe?"

"Look, I don't know him well enough to say for sure, but I think he had a lot on his mind. He made quite a splash recently as you know, and he copped a lot of criticism for the way he handled this business. I felt he was ... tired of it all, confused maybe. But not suicidal, if that's what you're thinking."

"No. We are treating it as homicide. You're certain there was nobody at the house when you were there?"

"Nobody I saw. No other vehicles besides his. Somebody must have arrived after I left."

"You are aware of his recent activities, the discovery of the bird and so on. Is there anything you can think of that could constitute a motive for murder?"

"Well, a lot of people were critical. But murder ... no, unless——"

"Yes?"

"Well, it's possible somebody wanted it badly enough to ... I mean his recording of the night parrot. That's how he got the bird to come in close to get photos."

"What value would the recording be, now that the discovery has already been made and documented in public?"

"It is only rumour and speculation but there are

always collectors looking for rare specimens. And right now, the night parrot is about the rarest thing on earth. The word is offers of over a million dollars are on the table for a clutch of eggs, maybe more for a live bird."

"And the way to get a live bird is with the recording?"

"That's how Elder found it."

Petersen finished writing. She gave him a long, non-committal look. "You're not planning to leave Cairns in the near future, are you, Mr. Butler?"

Butler returned his best neutral look. "No plans, no."

"In case I need to talk with you again, you understand. Here's my card if you think of anything else."

"Am I a suspect? Or have you found evidence of someone other than me at the scene?"

"I can't say right now, the SOCO's are still examining the house for evidence. But you're not being charged. Just stay in town, please."

As he emerged from the police station, Butler groped for a connection he had glimpsed in his mental replay of the visit to Elder's house. It was nothing that had been said, he was sure, but somewhere in the body language of that conversation, something more had been unwittingly communicated. He cursed the Drambuie. His recall was not up to the task, but he knew an important fragment had glistened for a second in his brain.

Learning to listen to the quiet currents of his mind

had taken him most of his life, not least because those close to him found his intuition eerily precise. Even Melissa had remarked she felt transparent around him, reassuring herself more than him that it was a good thing.

Handing the keys to Jake, he slumped into the passenger seat and tried to winkle out the fugitive thought.

"You okay, Ric?"

"Yeah, just trying to latch on to what might have been bothering Elder. Something was wrong; he was worried, and badly."

"You think he was expecting trouble to come knocking?"

"Maybe ... yeah. I can't see it clearly, but I feel he left me a clue that relates to his murder, and to the bird."

Jake gazed at Butler. "There's something about that bird with you, isn't there?"

Butler straightened in his seat as Jake started the car. He had to admit Jake's insight was sharper than his today. "I don't know, I've always been interested in it I guess, thought I might go searching for it myself someday ..."

"Yeah, right," said Jake, frowning.

Chapter 8

Butler drove a meandering route through the backblocks of Cairns, finding Jake's street pressed up against the towering paperbarks of the Central Swamp. He had lived all over Cairns in his time here but had almost forgotten these sulphurous suburbs, didn't know that parts of town were so unchanged. Even on this clear winter's day, the smell of the mangroves lay thick around the old fibro houses. He hadn't slept much and made an early start, only now realising it was an uncivilised hour to knock on Jake's door. Stopping to phone, he spied a wiry figure leaning on the fence up ahead, cup in hand, as if expecting him. He drew up alongside Jake.

"Where we going, boss?"

Butler snorted but smiled at Jake's gameness. "Hop in, Jake."

"I've left a message at the office that we'll be in late today," Butler explained as they headed south. "I need to catch up with James Marsh in Atherton. He was with Elder on a lot of his field trips. Maybe he knows what was going on out there."

"We trying to solve a murder now, boss?"

"No, but I think there's a connection between his death and the night parrot. I want to find out who knew about the bird or who most wanted to know. Elder was working on this for a long time, keeping it quiet, but somebody knew. Even before he announced his find, word leaked out that something big was happening in the trade, something in Australia. What else could it be? Someone has been planning to get a night parrot on the international market, I'm convinced of it."

Jake's face grew overcast. "Shame on us if we let that happen."

Butler's train of thought was derailed by the earnestness of Jake's concern. "We won't let it happen, mate," he promised, touching Jake's hand before his usual reserve could stop him. Jake squeezed his fingers and nodded. It was a minute before Butler reclaimed his hand, and another before he spoke again.

"There's a good chance Elder's killer is involved in a wildlife racket."

"Involved enough to kill him?"

"I don't know. There's a lot of money at stake and prestige for whoever could supply such a thing. Any serious dealer with a rich clientele would be salivating over this opportunity. And they need the one thing only Elder could provide."

"The recording! You're joking. They'd kill someone over a bird? How rare can they be? There's miles of spinifex country out there."

"Sure, but people have looked for it, good people,

and nobody's been able to find it for a hundred years. It could be like a lot of other desert animals, been pushed to near extinction by cats. It lives on the ground, and it's the right size prey for cats. For all we know, this could be the last one in existence."

"Surely there must be more—somewhere out there."

"Maybe, but nobody can say for sure. I'm not saying they planned to kill for it, but maybe Elder was unwilling. He was in a corner ... I'm sure that's the unease I saw in him."

Jake looked at him but said nothing.

They continued in silence past the Mulgrave River, crossed the Little Mulgrave, and began to climb. Jake's eyes softened as the mist-filled valley opened below them. Its imposing breadth was revealed as ranks of tree crowns loomed into view. He shook his head gently.

"Ric," he whispered, "whose country is this? I've never seen anything like it."

Butler nodded, glancing out as he drove the bends of the range. "I knew the old man who claimed this country—he called himself a magpie, a black bream—half black and half white. Been brought up the old way, in the bush. He's gone now. His people are still around but not many."

Jake's eyebrows rose appreciatively. "You know something then, Ric. You know a bit."

Jake gazed at the ever-widening valley and the mountain walls behind. Butler had viewed this scene many times, though not as broodingly ancient as it appeared this morning. Odd currents swirled below the mist, like stingray trails in sand. He felt the valley wash up against his skin, as lightly as Jake's touch had, as if his pores had been opened. He stole a look at Jake's hands.

They arrived at the top of the escarpment, breaking out of the forest into the crystal air of a tablelands morning. Atherton, nestled in the foothills of the Great Divide, was busier than Butler had ever seen it, the seething main street slowing traffic to a crawl. The bustle faded as they made their way to the narrow streets below Mount Baldy where Marsh's house backed onto dense bushland.

"I phoned him yesterday," said Butler, "but he sounded wary. He agreed to talk to me, but he might have gotten the impression I'm more senior than I am in the service, so we'll just run with that, okay?"

"Whatever you say, O Lord and Master," replied Jake drily, with a mischievous tilt of his head.

Marsh met them at the door. "Sorry to bother you, James, I'm sure you've had enough intrusions already, and sorry too about Jim. I gather you were good mates."

"Yeah, he was the best mate ... I've ever had, really," said Marsh, his eyes glazing.

"We wouldn't have come if it wasn't important."

"Right," said Marsh, gathering himself with obvious difficulty. "Come on in then."

He ushered them into the living room, the walls lined with photos of times out in the bush—Elder, Marsh, and others on saltpans, sand dunes, and by waterholes. It was a little shrine-like for Butler's taste, but one particular picture caught his eye.

"Great times," said Marsh. "Jim knew the most remarkable places. I never could work out how he could have visited so many places before and remember them all so well. He knew them intimately and the wildlife that lived there. He was astonishing."

"That he was," agreed Butler. "I met him many years ago and spent some time in the bush with him. He was the best naturalist I've ever met."

Marsh nodded, then shook his head in disbelief. "So how can I help you?" he asked, gesturing for them to sit down.

"Well, James, I'm hoping to find out who knew where you and Jim were working on this project; the night parrot. I know Jim was keeping the location quiet, but we're trying to establish how secure the spot is. Whether there's any chance of someone getting in there and disturbing the birds."

"Fair enough," said Marsh. "Then you understand I'm not at liberty to tell you where the site is. I can assure you only Jim and I were ever there. Obviously the station owner knows about it, but he's not about to let anyone else on there or publicise it. He was in complete agreement with Jim about keeping the location under wraps. Only a few people work full-time on the station and they didn't care what we were up to, provided the boss gave it his blessing. They knew we were doing something with wildlife, beyond that they weren't too curious. The owner has a way of surrounding himself with loyal staff. As far as I'm concerned, nobody else knew what we were doing. Even after Jim made his announcement the blokes working on the station weren't overly impressed, according to the owner. And he's as straight as they come, a good man."

Butler nodded while he jotted down a few notes. "I believe Jim had dropped clues over the last couple of years, once he started getting close—possibly once he had recorded the bird. A few rumours circulated that he was onto it."

"Sure, yeah, he told some of his more trusted friends and even some of his tour clients he was working on it and getting somewhere. But he was always careful not to name any places. He knew better than that."

"Well, I guess everyone realises now that it's in Queensland and roughly what part. Do you think anyone going down there could pick up local information about where you were working?"

"Not a chance. The station is a long way from the nearest town, and we rarely saw anyone in between. Even when we did, he would usually manage to avoid them—Jim was secretive—he loved the skulduggery actually, he was like a big kid that way. Anyone going down there would just find millions of acres of spinifex—like we did to begin with."

After a quarter of an hour of gentle probing, Butler was convinced he would get little change out of Marsh. He looked back at the photograph that had attracted his attention. The three people in the picture stood on purple-pink ground, and behind them was a tawny-dotted plain he was certain was spinifex. Elder and Marsh grinned at the camera, but the hefty third figure, with a more reserved expression, was unknown to him.

"Well, I think you've told us what we needed to

know, James. Thanks for your willingness to see us. Sorry again about Jim, I only hope you or someone can continue his work on the project."

"I haven't even thought about that to be honest. Still trying to get used to ... you know," he shrugged, his eyes moistening.

"Yeah." Butler stood to shake Marsh's hand. "It would have been great to spend so much time out bush with Jim. He was quite a character."

"He certainly was."

"Before I go, James, can you help me place that face in the picture?"

"Oh, that's Col Stringer. Doctor Col, as Jim always called him. We used to run into him a bit out in that country. He worked for the museum in Brisbane, Jim said, doing some kind of research near the town we'd go to for supplies. That's where we'd see him usually. He turned up too often for my liking, but Jim wasn't worried, said he was a typical academic that wouldn't have a clue what we were doing. Jim didn't have much time for academics, but he got on all right with Col, always had time for a private chat with him. I like that photo because we were on our way home after we first recorded the bird. We had a new secret—a bird call nobody else had ever heard."

Butler's desk had been piled with paperwork by the time he arrived, late morning. It seemed he was now the office archivist with documents stretching back a decade to be reviewed and re-classified. Weagle's accompanying memo was written obtusely but made it clear this work was to take priority over any fieldwork Butler had planned. He shoved the papers away from his blotter, found Jake a chair, and asked him to look busy. Meanwhile, he surfed the internet for Dr Col Stringer. It took longer than expected to find a connection between Stringer and the Queensland Museum, but opening the twenty-year-old document that had been scanned into their database puzzled him even further. Stringer was listed as a research fellow, but his expertise was described as brackish wetlands. Perhaps his field of study had changed and the database hadn't been updated. An hour later, Butler had found only older references to Stringer. The only photograph he had found, from a museum report, was difficult to reconcile with the picture seen at Marsh's house. The young, clean-shaven man in the report bore little resemblance to the waxen-faced and grey-bearded man standing on the spinifex plain.

Butler worked through the lunch break before deciding to drop an email to an old university pal who had worked at the museum since graduating. Ten minutes later, Billy Baker phoned and Butler realised with a grin it had been an era since they had spoken.

"Ric, it's Billy. Listen, I can't talk long. DNA is on the stove but, hey man, it's good to hear from you. The guy you're after, Stringer, he worked here when I started, but he hasn't been here for at least twenty years ... he stopped coming to work mysteriously, but who knows what happened. There were rumours he did something, I don't want to say illegal, but something not good ... I can try to find out more."

"Thanks, Billy, that would be great. How are——"

"Okay. Hey, gotta go, great to hear from you, man."
Click.

"You too, Billy," laughed Butler as he put down his
phone. He peered over the pile of papers at Jake, who
was less amused at how the day had turned out. "I need
some lunch, Ric. I'm fed up with this end of the job."

Outside the building, Butler enlightened Jake on
the most recent revelation. "I can't believe Stringer
convinced Elder he still worked at the museum. Elder
knew most or all of the birding community including
the museum people, and twenty years ago that was a
small community. So why did Elder tell Marsh this guy
still worked there?"

"Could he be at one of the other museums? Maybe
Marsh got it wrong."

"I thought of that, but he's not coming up in any
searches. It's almost like he disappeared from the
face of the earth; not a single recent reference to him
anywhere. I mean it's hard to keep a profile as low as
this guy these days. Even you're on the internet, Jake."

"What? How do you know?"

Butler shrugged. "I looked you up after you came
to work with me. It's good to have a bit of background
information. There wasn't much by the way."

Jake took Butler's elbow. "Ric, I know everyone
uses the net these days, but ... could you talk to me if
you want to know anything, please?" Hurt simmered in
his eyes.

"Yeah ... okay. Sorry, I meant no offence."

"Don't worry about it. So, what do you think was

going on with this Stringer character?"

Feeling as if he had missed some nuance, Butler gathered his thoughts. "I don't know ... something out of the ordinary. I hoped Stringer might lead us to where Elder was working, maybe give some insight into how secret the parrot site really is. But it looks as if Stringer is the secretive one. He dropped out of sight years ago, and there must be a reason for it. And yet he remained in touch with Elder regularly. Something's not adding up."

Chapter 9

Butler tossed and turned for most of the night. Every time he closed his eyes the spinifex-dotted plain appeared, with the face of Dr Col dissolving in a heat haze. When he opened them, the turmoil merely shifted to his new offsider. He felt an easy affinity with Jake, as if an unknown providence bound them together. He could still feel his hand squeezed, as if by someone he had known for a long time. He didn't like to be touched; making only rare exceptions for lovers and select old friends. Yet Jake's touch fitted, like a brother's, or at least how he imagined it. But there was something in Jake's manner that bothered him. Seeing the distress on his face, he had been genuinely remorseful about searching Jake's name but the hurt had flickered too quickly to forgiveness, as if trading guilt. Surely, he was being paranoid ... but it was unlike him to feel such trust so quickly. He closed his eyes again, finding it easier to float disembodied above the spinifex.

He got up and made coffee about 4am, knowing he would not sleep, and fired up the internet. Col

Stringer's name continued to draw a blank. His early career was documented: a BSc and PhD at the University of Queensland, a postdoctoral fellowship in limnology, and a series of publications marking his arrival as a scientist, followed by a permanent job at the museum. Then the trail hit stony ground.

He sat back with his coffee and tried to imagine how a career scientist could disappear so completely while maintaining an active field project in the Southwest. The funding for fieldwork had to come from somewhere ... and permits would have been granted by the bureaucracy he knew so well. Two hours of intensive search later, no research records were found, current or during the past decade. Stringer was a phantom, every bit as much as the night parrot. And Elder was the link, if there was one. He must have known Stringer was no longer a museum researcher, so why continue to say he was? Whatever Stringer's line of work was now, Elder had been hiding it. But why? And was this related to the whiff of fear Butler detected on that Sunday?

He stepped onto his small patio, his eyes drawn to the layered silhouettes of wild gingers and fan palms he had planted in the bottom of his sloping backyard. The rising sun, greeted with gusto by the brown honeyeaters, bathed the garden in a rosy glow. A V-shaped formation of ibises, their necks outstretched, emerged from the line of tall paperbarks beyond. Deep draughts of the mild tropical air loosened his body and restored his eyes after too many hours in front of a computer screen. His phone rang, interrupting the reverie. Glancing at his watch, he realised it was almost seven. Still, it felt too early for a phone call.

"Hello."

"Ric, it's Billy. Sorry, I know it's early, man, but I have a big day. Listen, I found out more about your man Stringer ... a couple of the old-timers here remember him well. One of them ... do you need names? I hope not. One reckons he was mixed up in some dodgy dealings ... like passing information to traffickers stealing bird eggs, you know rare birds, endangered even ... using museum records to tip them off about the nest's whereabouts. So he got fired ... but get this ... he had some kind of leverage, so it was never publicised and he wasn't prosecuted. All kept hush hush, you know what I mean? Sorry, dude, the gels are calling, hope that's helpful." Click.

Butler's phone hand dropped to his side as the Stringer mystery simultaneously unravelled and deepened. Billy's information had left him gobsmacked. The connection with illegal bird dealing could not be a coincidence.

Sitting at his Parks office desk, Butler retrieved Eileen Petersen's card from those floating about in his top drawer. He glanced around to make sure he still had the office to himself and hastily dialled her number. She answered with the arctic efficiency he expected.

"Hi, Eileen, Ric Butler here."

"Mr Butler. How can I help you?"

He grimaced.

"Eileen, I'm calling with information relating to Jim Elder."

"Something you forgot to mention in our interview?"

"More like something I've since discovered."

"What is it?"

He braced himself.

"It could be related to the theft of the recording."

"Yes?"

Bingo. Quid pro quo was easy when you knew how.

"A Dr Col Stringer, formerly of the Queensland Museum, was an associate of Elder's, and in regular contact with him leading up to his murder. Through an old colleague, I've learned he has been involved in illegal bird dealing in the past. A coincidence, don't you think? At the very least he could shed light on Elder's recent activities and contacts."

He could almost hear Petersen's mind ticking.

"How did you discover a connection between Elder and Stringer?"

"James Marsh. He had a picture of the three of them together ... said Elder and Stringer were mates. I made a few enquiries from there."

"That's all?"

"Pretty much."

"Thank you, Mr Butler."

"Can I ask you a question, Eileen?"

"Go ahead."

"Do you have any leads yet?"

"I'm not at liberty to say, Mr Butler." He heard her voice thaw a little. "Thank you for the information. Have a good day."

"You too, Eileen."

Bingo! The recording had been stolen. He had gambled on first-name familiarity with Petersen to catch her off guard, suspecting she wasn't accustomed to men using her first name. Even so, he had heard the hesitation in her voice. Maybe she realised she'd divulged too much but made no comment, hoping he couldn't be devious enough to notice. He felt guilty but also confident Petersen would unearth more about Stringer, details he wanted to find out.

Now he had to work out Jake's story. First a stroll to the flame trees cafe. While he waited for his coffee, he made notes on his recent discoveries. Tapping his pen on the page, he gazed upwards. The first flush of bright, red bell-shaped flowers emerged from the branches above him. Words from his mother's gentle voice flooded his mind.

"Flame trees remind me of when I was a girl. That red colour is the same as a beautiful flower from my father's country."

Butler was young, maybe ten years old. It was one of the few clues he had about her, and it came to him every year with the blossoming. He had no memory of his grandfather but imagined him sitting outside a seaside cottage beneath a red-flowering tree. His mother had artfully deflected his teenage interrogations until he just accepted the hidden part of her life. It was a secret that urged her to spy up and down the street before leaving for work each night. In time he stopped asking.

Walking along the laneway that led back to his office, he saw Jake enter the building. What was it that bothered him about his new offsider? Butler stopped dead. Jake's rakish form knocked on Weagle's door. What the hell? He waited, squeezed between two parked cars and strained to see through Weagle's window. Again, he felt guilty, but the guilt turned to disbelief as more minutes passed. Weagle had no time for underlings. What could he possibly have to talk to Jake about?

A full fifteen minutes later, Butler walked into his office and sat down beside Jake. "Hi, Jake, been waiting long?"

"No, just got here," fibbed Jake as he pretended to be engrossed in old files. He looked up and smiled.

"Don't get too absorbed. I want to get out of here by lunchtime so I can see Marsh again."

"Sounds good, boss."

Learning that Weagle was busy in meetings for most of the day, Butler made his excuses and escaped by late morning. Soon they were driving up the escarpment again; this time the river glittered through the sun-drenched canopy.

"So, Jake, how do you get on with Weagle?"

"You don't like him much, do you?"

"He'd be happy if I wasted the rest of my career on those files." Jake shifted and glanced out the window.

"I saw you come out of his office this morning, Jake. What was that about?"

Jake hesitated. "Asking if I was settling in all right, you know?"

"No, I don't know. You tell me."

"That was about it, Ric."

"Listen, Jake. Is there something I should know about?"

"Nope, nothing mate." Butler sensed Jake's unease despite his efforts not to show it.

Outside Marsh's house, Butler placed his hand on Jake's shoulder.

"Sit tight, Jake. Only one of us needs to go in there."

Jake looked startled, like a shoplifting kid caught with lollies under his jumper. He composed himself. "Uh, okay ... no worries, boss."

Marsh answered the door, clearly not expecting Butler this time. Ten minutes later, Butler jumped back into the car.

"Find out anything useful?" asked Jake.

"Listen, Jake, I need to know what's going on with you and Weagle. I like you, mate, but I don't trust Weagle one bit. You were in his office for longer than it would take for him to ask how you're settling in, even if he would do that."

Jake's shoulders slumped. "I'm sorry, I shouldn't have lied to you."

"So, what was the chit-chat about?"

"Ric, I like you too and you seem like a decent bloke, and there haven't been that many—not to me, anyway."

"And?"

"And Weagle had me cornered. I have to keep him informed about what you're doing, otherwise he'll ... fire me."

"You've been going behind my back this whole time?"

"No, I haven't, Ric. I told him you've been trying to find leads on the bird, but getting nowhere——"

"That doesn't take fifteen minutes."

"I told him nothing, I swear. I made up bullshit. I

can bullshit pretty well, Ric ... when I need to, I mean."

"I want to believe you, Jake, but——" Butler's phone rang. He ignored it until he saw it was Melissa's name that lit the screen. She was the last person he expected to hear from. He climbed from the cab and answered.

"Hi, Meliss ... How have you been?"

"Listen, Ric. Have you heard from anyone in the office in the last hour?"

"No, why?"

"Because the rumour is you're involved in Elder's murder and on the run. Ric, the police are after you for questioning."

"What the hell! Are you sure about this, Meliss? I've only ducked out of the office for the afternoon."

"I don't believe it either. But it sounds as if someone here has dobbed you in. Saying your visit to Elder wasn't officially approved."

"Weagle!"

"I don't know, but you need to go to the police and sort it out."

"Thanks, Meliss. I have to go."

"Okay, Ric, but whatever you do, don't run."

A stomach-churning dread washed over Butler and he leaned on the car. He felt a hand on his shoulder and turned to see Jake's concerned face.

"Are you okay, Ric?"

Chapter 10

In far South West Queensland, a Landcruiser ute crawled across the plain as the shadows of spinifex clumps lengthened. A bulky figure hung precariously out of the cab, where the driver's side door had been removed, and watched the ground.

The vehicle abruptly stopped, and the bearded occupant got out and strode back a few steps. Checking a GPS, he dropped the tailgate and pulled out poles, rope, and a canvas backpack. Working quickly, he paced out a wide semi-circle, dropping poles at twelve-metre intervals. Staking out the last pole with pegs and rope, he pulled a calico bag from the backpack and began to unfold the tightly-wadded black ball inside.

Teasing out the net into a fine mesh, he raised the base of the pole and slid on a set of loops from one end of the net. He walked backwards to the next pole, humming a Bach symphony as he went. After checking the tension and staking the second pole, he set another net, artfully alternating the loops with those of the first. Like a Zulu impi outflanking its enemy, he erected a two-metre high net wall that half-encircled a hundred metre swathe of old spinifex. In the dwindling light, the net was close to invisible.

Returning the backpack to the truck, he took out a smaller leather bag and carefully opened it to remove a pair of compact black speakers. Connecting a finger-sized device to one speaker, he scanned the ground from left to right until he chose an ideal spot. He drove a shorter pole into the ground, fastening the speakers to small brackets and nursing the device in his hand. Pressing a button, he smiled as a high-pitched piping call played, clear and loud, carrying across the plain. Satisfied, he strolled back to the ute, opened a bottle of red wine, and waited beneath a reddening sky.

Chapter 11

Butler sat in the dark—pondering what his next move should be. Weagle's police connections were as all-pervading as a pumpkin vine, which ruled out the local watch house as an option. Certain that he was being set up, he saw little point in entering the lion's den. He needed to ride out the storm, but how big the storm was or how long it would rage he didn't know.

In the near distance an orange firefly glowed periodically—Jake smoking a cigarette at the end of the yard. Bob's bush depot just outside Mount Molloy had been the closest thing Butler could find to a hideout. Rented to store Bob's field equipment, the large rickety shed housed two vehicles and a row of metal cupboards full of gear. Bob had instantly offered the premises, informing the owner that a colleague would camp overnight and use the equipment.

"You're not worried about being an accessory, Bob?" asked Butler, concerned his predicament had left Bob with little choice.

"You're no criminal, mate. Stay as long as you

need, take whatever you want and let me know what else I can do to help. I'll find out what I can about Stringer. If you can get here, you know you're welcome to stay at the house."

The thought of spending time with Bob was enticing, but driving to the city was unsafe. If his situation worsened, the last thing he needed was to further implicate Bob.

Weagle had advanced beyond spiteful this time. What could motivate him to implicate Butler ... unless ...? Why would Weagle feel threatened by him? It didn't make any sense. Butler thanked the heavens his mother was not alive to see his face plastered over newspapers and TV.

On the car radio, the Majestic Fanfare tune announced the beginning of the ABC's news bulletin. His disappearance had made the top local story. He climbed into the driver's seat and turned up the volume.

The newscaster began: "In today's news, an arrest warrant has been issued for Ric Butler, an employee of Queensland National Parks and Wildlife, in relation to the murder of the renowned naturalist, Jim Elder. Assisting him in evading police is an accomplice of slim build, average height and dark complexion."

"Dark, my arse!" Jake's voice boomed from the darkness. "I'm black, you bastards. Shit! I'm an accomplice now, am I?"

Butler groaned, swamped by an increasing sense of helplessness.

Jake yanked open the passenger side door, the

dash lights catching his cheekbones as he leapt in. "Ric, we have to get out of here. This is too close to Cairns."

"Jake, you heard what they said. They think you're an accomplice. You have to hand yourself in."

"You're joking, mate. Weagle wants your head and now he's after mine. He's the one feeding the coppers this malarkey. His cronies will crucify us if we turn ourselves in; you because you're a thorn in his side, and me cos I'm black."

"That's crazy, Jake. Why would he go to this much trouble to get rid of me? He could have come up with any trumped-up bullshit to fire me if he wanted to."

"He's hiding something, Ric, and you're getting too close. Can't you see?"

"Weagle's an arsehole but mixed up in murder? Bloody hell, Jake, this is doing my head in. I don't know what to think!"

"Can you imagine a more untrustworthy arsehole? Of course, he's bent!"

Butler's head sank to the steering wheel. Jake must be right. Weagle was the epitome of a corrupt official, a self-satisfied megalomaniac sporting a Rolex. For the past decade, Butler had been so busy staying out of Weagle's way he never thought to delve deeper into his boss's affairs. Weagle certainly overstepped his privileges and was predictably inefficient, but was he deliberately hamstringing the fauna squad's policing work?

"Ric?" Jake's voice was calmer now. "We have to move now while it's dark. There's a place we can go a long way from here, my family's place. We'll be safe there until this blows over."

Butler turned on the cab light so he could see Jake's face. Jake gave an urgent nod, his face pleading. "Come on, mate, let's get moving."

Chapter 12

At first light, the university's Hilux approached the Diamantina headwaters. They had skirted the few sizeable towns on the tablelands and dropped onto the dark plains of central Queensland. The Parks vehicle abandoned on a bush track near Mount Molloy, might help give the impression they were headed north. Having driven through most of the night, Jake dozed.

Butler stared ahead at the sunrise as he drove. The low golden light gilded the crests of the landscape, setting them afloat above the purple shadows of the lower ground. He dimly registered the beauty of the vista, his mind numbed by the nightmare of the past eighteen hours. Seeing the road ahead more clearly, he increased his speed.

He stopped at the top of a rocky rise where he placed the billy on the small Metho stove. He envied Jake's ability to sleep at a time like this. His own brain trawled over the events of yesterday, replaying each until more questions than answers filled his head and he had to start over again. He hoped his mind would clear after a shot of caffeine.

Jake tumbled out of the truck after a few minutes. "God, it's good to be out here, eh? Away from all the crap. Sorry, mate, you look buggered."

"I love it out here, Jake, but yeah ... shattered. I can't believe I'm a bloody fugitive."

"You and me both, mate. Coffee smells good. Where are we?"

"We snuck through Hughenden just before dawn, so I reckon we're halfway to Winton. We'll need fuel by then, but it might be best if just one of us goes into town."

"I'll go. They're mainly looking for you. I won't get too much attention."

"How much cash have you got?"

"Enough to fill up. But they have eftpos here now, you know," he teased.

"The police will be all over us like flies if we use cards. Take that wad of cash I got in Atherton yesterday and fill the jerries too."

"You're a better fugitive than I am, mate."

"Ha! Make yourself useful, will you. There's powdered milk in there somewhere."

Chapter 13

Weagle's claim that Butler was on the run and involved in Elder's murder surprised Eileen Petersen. His vehement finger-pointing, which in her professional opinion lacked substance, was suspiciously reminiscent of a corrupt 1980s Queensland. It seemed to her the rude and leering chief of the fauna squad had an axe to grind.

Her sharply honed investigatory skills, courtesy of a dedicated father who worked as a QC during the seventies, meant Weagle would need more than an executive office and an overbearing attitude to convince her. His cause wasn't helped by his misogynist tendencies. But that would have to wait.

Petersen could not reconcile Weagle's testimony with her impression of Butler. She had also spoken with Gordon Prescott who raised the possibility of Butler being mixed up in wildlife trafficking, but this made even less sense to Petersen.

Driving back into town, she dissected the events of the past few days. Butler's behaviour during the

airport bust sounded unusual, as was his ill-timed visit
to Elder's house. But the suggestion he was involved in
smuggling, let alone murder, didn't fit with the quiet
loathing she detected in Butler when they spoke about
wildlife collectors. Although she couldn't join all the
dots now, she was convinced Butler was no murderer.
Her police academy mentor would have shuddered at
her disregard for "... the evidence, the evidence!", but
her father would have applauded her instincts.

Petersen had moved almost 1800 kilometres north
of the capital to take up her position in Cairns, but
to her the location more than compensated for the
isolation. The police station overlooked the tropical
coastline, and she never tired of the view—rainforest-
covered hills sweeping south to the highest mountains
in Queensland. It had taken a little longer to get
accustomed to the heat. Walking through the heavy
glass doors into the air-conditioned station, Petersen
found a dark-haired woman waiting in reception.

"Hello, I'm Senior Constable Petersen. Can I help
you?"

"Melissa Fraser. I work at National Parks. It's about
Ric Butler." Her voice wavered.

"Please, step into my office."

Petersen closed the door of her spare and spotless
office. Melissa took a seat.

"Miss Fraser, you work with Mr Butler?"

"Yes ... No ... It's more than that. We were together
until recently."

"Until he disappeared?"

"No. Before that. I know this is probably out of

line, but I wanted to ask if there is any word from him."

Petersen tried to frame a response that was both professional and sympathetic, but for once her mind was strangely at odds with her well-organised desk. "I can't disclose any information, I'm afraid."

"Oh. I'm sorry. I shouldn't have bothered you."

Melissa's slender fingers pressed into the skin of her forearms and her eyes glimmered with watery tears. As she stood to leave, she blurted out, "It's just that someone is trying to implicate Ric in Elder's murder. I'm positive he isn't involved."

Petersen nodded, hoping her eyes showed the same gentle concern her fathers used to. "You think somebody might have it in for him?"

"It's possible. Ric is more idealistic than most of the people he works with. He's passionate about what he does, but he has principles. He would never hurt anybody."

"Is there anyone in particular who dislikes him?"

Melissa hesitated, then nodded firmly. "His boss."

"Karl Weagle?"

Melissa nodded again. "I'm sorry. I've probably said too much."

"Thank you for coming in, Miss Fraser," said Petersen.

"Please, call me Melissa. Can you let me know if he is safe?"

"It's an ongoing investigation, so I can't promise anything. But hopefully it will all be sorted out soon." Petersen was acutely aware how inadequate her answer sounded. "I'm sure he'll be in touch."

Melissa frowned. "Maybe. But keeping in touch was never his strong point."

As Melissa strode through the doorway, Petersen felt vindicated that she wasn't the only person to harbour suspicions about Weagle. But even if he was the boss from hell, it didn't change the truth. Butler had run. The million-dollar question was, where to and why?

Chapter 14

Jake arrived back from town with a topped-up fuel tank and two full jerry cans. He cautiously stepped over Butler who lay snoring in the sparse shade with a scorching midday sun directly overhead.

"Ric," he whispered, wishing he didn't have to disturb the only sleep the bloke had had in a couple of days. "We've got to go, Ric," a bit louder now.

Butler woke in a flurry of limbs, falling over himself as he tried to get up, dust sticking to the spittle on his cheek as he tangled himself in mulga branches.

"Ric, it's me!"

"Shit, Jake, you should know better than to sneak up on someone like that."

"You were asleep."

Butler's heart pounded, his breathing hard and involuntarily deep.

"Sorry, Jake, I was dreaming. That bastard Weagle caught up to me, he found me. I was paralysed; I couldn't move or speak, even though he was about to kill me."

"It's okay. We're a long way from him here. We're safe."

Jake drove, but Butler, despite his exhaustion, couldn't sleep. The feeling of impending doom from his dream stayed with him. He expected to feel safer as they pushed on southwest, far from any towns, but he still felt shadowed. Not even the first sign of spinifex could lighten his heart.

"We'll be there this evening, Ric. We'll be right once we get there, you'll see."

By late afternoon they were beyond Diamantina Gates and pushing towards the treeless plains of Mitchell Grass country. Jake needed a spell, and Butler badly needed a break from the dread crushing in on him.

"Jake, you're tired. Let's stop and make a cuppa, then I'll drive for a bit. We must be close."

"Yeah, not far now. Another hour, an hour and a half, tops."

On the sunlit plain, a million miles from anywhere it seemed, Jake set up the stove.

"Give me a yell when the billy has boiled," called Butler, not wanting to leave the truck or move his tired limbs until he absolutely had to. His eyes closed, as sleep beckoned. He began to drift, unconscious and grateful. *No, no, I mustn't sleep yet ...* he woke with a start, confused to hear the distant-sounding bleep of a mobile phone going flat. It could only be Jake's. But why was it turned on? He rummaged through Jake's bag for the phone. The screen displayed a call made a few hours earlier. Butler gripped the phone, breathing deeply to stop himself from smashing it into the dashboard. Jake had called Weagle's phone number several times over the past week.

Jake looked up from the stove to see Butler marching towards him. His phone caught him on the hip, stinging from the ferocity of a powerful throw. He scrambled to his feet just as Butler launched his full weight at him, tackling him to the ground. Winded, Jake took two lashing blows before he freed his arms and made a grab for Butler's throat.

"What are you doing, Ric? Stop it!"

Another hit, this time a hard slap to the temple. Butler was no fighter, but he was mightily enraged, striking out blindly.

"You double-crossing shit, you've been on the phone to Weagle. I knew there was something going on with you and him. So, you're his boy, and you're playing me for a fool. Where are we really going, eh?"

A knee to the groin, this time it hurt. Jake pushed back, throwing Butler off balance easily, and smashing the ball of his hand into his solar plexus. He wriggled away as Butler fell on his side struggling for breath.

"Ric, listen. Stop——"

"You murri bastard ...," heaved Butler.

"Ric, it's not what you think. Weagle is no friend of mine. Listen to me!"

Butler, still short of breath, managed a weak groan.

"He forced me to inform on you. But I've been bullshitting him. He thinks we're heading west, towards the Gulf."

"Why should I believe you? How could he have that hold over you?"

"It's a long story, but I'll tell you this—and this is the honest truth. When Weagle was a cop out our way, years ago, my father witnessed his involvement in some nasty stuff. Weagle has been leaning on my family ever since, desperate to keep his dirty laundry out of sight. Every time he thinks we need a reminder he has the local coppers pick up my grandad. They keep the poor old bugger in a cell until we come begging. He's eighty now, half blind, and they're still harassing him. My father used to do whatever dirty work Weagle or his mates needed, now it's me. You don't know what it's like out here, Ric, it's the law of the bloody jungle."

"Come on, it's the twenty-first century now. There are ways to protect yourself against that sort——"

"What would you know, Ric! Especially about family."

It rang painfully true.

"Jake, I know it's——"

"Don't bloody patronise me! You just called me a murri bastard. That's rich, Ric, coming from you."

"What the hell do you mean by that?"

"You're in denial of who you are mate. It was obvious as soon as I laid eyes on you."

Butler reeled back as if expecting a blow. "You're losing it, mate."

"Fuck you, Ric. How the hell did you get that name?"

"What the ...?"

"It's a bit *unusual*, that's all."

The dark eyes were mocking now.

"I saw your driver's licence, Ricardo Harrison Butler. Did you think you had an ethnic background or something? Spanish maybe? Either that or your mum watched Fantasy Island every week. Yeah, all the mums loved Ricardo Montalban, eh?"

Fantasy Island—the Saturday night ritual of his childhood. How could Jake know it was his mother's favourite TV show?

"Harrison ... what year were you born again? Yeah, that's right; the same year *Star Wars* came out. Lucky, she didn't name you Chewbacca, mate!"

"I've got no idea what you're on about, Jake."

"You'll see soon enough. That photo in your wallet, I've got a dozen cousins that look just like your mother. Half of them are called Butler too."

Butler looked through Jake as if something stood a mile behind him.

"Come on, Ric!"

Butler blinked, returning to the present, still unable to grasp what Jake was saying.

"You mean you haven't worked it out? You've got a murri name, mate. Your mother was a murri."

Jake started back towards the truck, stopped and turned.

"You're a murri, Ric. Get used to it."

Chapter 15

Petersen had had little success in finding information on Col Stringer, the former museum worker, until she turned to James Marsh. Doctor Col, as Marsh called him, was an enigma, but he always seemed keen to buttonhole Elder. Marsh remained on the outer, forced to wait around in dusty one-horse towns for the two to wrap up their private conversations, and could not recall Elder ever divulging the subject of their long chats. The only lead he supplied was the name of an aviculturist he had heard during one of their bush trips—Graham Flanagan. From the sound of it, Flanagan knew both Elder and Stringer. Finally a connection. Stringer's invisibility unsettled Petersen, but intuition told her he played a key part in this murder.

Chapter 16

As Butler drove west ahead of the dusk, his spirit drifted on the wind, the vehicle a pale speck on the curving red landscape below. Each time he descended towards his body, he met a stony resistance, as though the man driving was curled in on himself—foetus-like. The hands, clenched in place on the wheel, made no attempt to avoid the potholes, each impact sending a bone-shattering shudder through the cab.

Jake sat silent, casting sidelong glances at him, and flinching with each jolt.

A flock of small birds flickered up off the road, scraps of light against the sinking sun. Blinded by the glare, Butler reacted seconds too late, swinging the wheel wildly. The vehicle lurched off the road and ploughed through a thicket of gidgee, until the biggest trunk brought it to a neck-jarring halt. Butler's head smashed against the wheel.

"Ric!"

Blood oozed from the wound.

"Aw shit, Ric, are you okay?"

With one hand covered in blood and his face purple with rage, Butler growled as he unclipped his seat belt and kicked his way out the door. He limped back onto the road, cursing himself.

Jake followed. "It's okay, no harm done. We'll have the truck back on the road in a minute."

The day, in all its rawness and confusion, flailed again at Butler. The sunset was merciless, ferocious in its beauty, but it was the jewel-like body on the road that undid him. He fell to his knees in the dirt, his head dropping and his shoulders convulsing with sobs. He picked up the perfect but lifeless bird, a tear washing the dust from its tiny orange feet.

By the time he laid the zebra finch to rest under a shrub, the bird's feathers were matted with salty moisture. Turning to Jake, who had sat quietly by the car, he felt his damp face crease. "It's been a long day, Jake. I know you're keen to see your family, but I can't face anyone tonight. Do you mind if we camp here?"

"That's okay, Ric. It's getting too dark to see what we're doing now anyway."

"Thanks. I mean it."

Cocooned in the protective embrace of his swag, Butler's mind stopped revolving. Even the gravel felt like down under his weary bones. As he drifted into sleep, his battered body was lulled by a slow, rhythmic drone that seemed to vibrate into his feet from the earth, soothing his limbs, his heart, and passing out the crown of his head towards the stars.

He woke sometime in the moonless night, rolling onto his back to gaze up into the broad sweep of the

Milky Way. Reaching out to touch the dirt with one hand, he realised the inland had worked its magic; his stomach was calm, his shoulders soft. The drama of North Queensland played out in a parallel world, another life to which he never needed to return. Jake was right, he was safe out here. And that was all he needed for now.

Chapter 17

Graham Flanagan was easy to track down—he lived in Innisfail—but a little harder to contact. After two days of phone messages, he had finally returned Petersen's call and agreed to an interview. Now, as she pulled off the highway at Goondi Bend and cruised along a lane lined with ramshackle Queenslanders, she saw a strange, wool-hatted figure crouching at the first corner. It was a clear, hot day—granted in what passed for winter around here, but close to thirty degrees. Flanagan's Himalayan ear warmer suffocated his entire head. He stood as she slowed down next to him and he pointed down the street. After seven years in Cairns, the eccentricity of North Queenslanders still befuddled her.

"Park by the yellow fence," he said with a deep frown.

"Would you like a lift?" she asked awkwardly. It was only fifty metres away.

"No, that's all right, I'll get there by the time you're out of the car," he replied.

She pulled up alongside the fence, noticing the mailbox had numbered digits almost a foot high. She wondered why he had insisted she might have trouble finding the place.

By the time she collected her notebook and bag, he was standing to attention beside her front bumper bar.

"Graham Flanagan," he said, unnecessarily. "Lovely day."

"Um, yes. I'm Senior Constable Eileen Petersen, Cairns CIB."

"Right. I was going to phone you, you know."

"Sorry?"

"After he was killed, I mean. I felt I should ... talk to you."

Petersen was a little confused. "I see. What about, exactly?"

"Well, I thought I should—what do they say—assist with your enquiries."

She wondered if Flanagan was ready to conduct the interview on the footpath.

"Yes, well, thank you. And I hope you can help us. Perhaps ..." she motioned towards the house.

"Oh, yes, of course. But I don't live here."

"Where *do* you live?"

"Across the road."

"Ah, right. Shall we?"

She eyed a high numberless fence which overflowed with thick shrubbery that virtually hid the house.

He glanced furtively up and down the street. "Yes,

okay then. Quickly." Seeing her bemused expression, he added, "It's the New Caledonians. Highly sought-after. Can't be too careful."

Her research on the case had educated her enough to know he was referring to some parrots.

He led her through an elaborately bolted gate and paused to reset the alarm system. Safely within his walled compound, he relaxed enough to remove his headgear and show her to an outdoor setting surrounded by aviaries.

"It was Orcherton," he said, sitting down opposite her.

"I beg your pardon?"

"Dick Orcherton. He's the one you need to talk to. He's a breeder and trader, and he had a strong interest in Jim Elder's doings. In fact, he pumped me for information on Elder any chance he got. An unhealthy interest I would say."

"Just a minute, please. This Orcherton was asking you for information on Elder's activities? And you had that sort of information?"

"Oh, yes. Jim was always keen to let someone know what he was up to. Couldn't keep a secret if his life depended on it—oh, sorry. But he was one of those blokes who just had to tell you what he was doing, how he was almost on to the ultimate rare bird. The night parrot, of course."

Petersen's head spun. "Okay, can we backtrack a little, please? When did you first hear about Elder's interest in the night parrot?"

"Oh, years ago. Maybe ten, fifteen years. He was

always keen—like all of us. Just the mystery of it, you know. But I knew he was determined to find it at least twelve years ago. Well before the headless body showed up."

"Wait. A headless body showed up?"

"Yes. The headless carcass of the parrot was found out at Diamantina strung up on a barbwire fence."

"Oh, okay. Please go on."

"Well, Jim was the only person I knew who methodically searched for it. Then, maybe five years ago, he phoned me one night, all excited, said he had heard the thing way out west somewhere. After that, he was out bush all the time, really chasing it. I thought he'd give up like everyone else, but he stuck at it. He spoke to me once in a while about how he had heard it again, but he was no closer, then suddenly he dropped in here one day, buzzing like a march fly. He had managed to record the damn thing. I was flabbergasted. I mean it was only a matter of time and by God he did it, the bugger."

"And how long have you known Orcherton?"

"Oh, a long time. Maybe twenty years. He comes and goes. But he's been in touch more often over the last few years, mainly to do with this night parrot business. He was out to ... gazump Jim, I suppose."

"And he knew you had information?"

"Yes."

Flanagan drew a breath and sat back. He looked like a man ready to unburden himself. She gave him a moment to collect his thoughts.

"Well, look, it was ... circumstances."

Flanagan looked like a caged parrot with the walls closing in. She leaned back to give him a little more space.

He nodded to himself.

"Jim and I grew up together and we were good mates. We were competitive about collecting from since I can remember. He'd show off the snake he'd bagged, and I'd pull out a goanna, that sort of thing. At home we had finches, then bigger birds, parrots and all the rest. We were always out in the scrub, trying to catch a Wompoo or get hold of something rare. It was fun, you know, but competitive too. And he always had to be the best. Bloody taipans ... and once he got a car, he was away up the Cape bringing back eclectus parrots and so on. He started to make a name for himself; supplying breeders down south. I mean I was still into it, but he left the rest of us for dead. Loved to crow about it too."

His eyes shifted to the side and became glassy. He squirmed in his seat and asked, "Would you like a cup of tea, coffee?"

"No, thank you. I know this must be difficult for you, please continue." Petersen feared he was about to cry. "When you're ready."

"That's why he used to call me about his night parrot trips. He had to crow about it to somebody. He was brilliant, you know—in the bush, I mean. Nobody could touch him. But he always had to brag about his exploits; wanted recognition, I suppose. And after the ... errors of judgement, he seemed to need reassuring even more."

"Errors?"

"Yes. He got a bit carried away at times, made some dubious claims. I think he was desperate to be taken seriously by the establishment. Funnily he always said they were worthless—the scientists, the government departments—but he still seemed to need their approval. I reckon he thought this night parrot discovery would do it for him; seal him as the greatest. He was very careful about getting the goods before he made any claims. But he had to tell someone. And the closer he got the more excited he was, the more he would tell me. He didn't want to give much away, but he wanted to taunt me too, by giving me little clues about where it was. He knew I wanted to know, so he'd tell me something more each time just so I knew he was for real, but not enough information for me to look myself. I think he still considered us rivals of some kind. Me! I mean, why should he care. He never took me seriously, but he strung me along all the same."

Flanagan sat back and shook his head slowly.

"And Orcherton?"

Flanagan's lip quivered as he spoke. "Orcherton used to call me once in a while."

"Please, go on."

"Well, it was mainly about buying birds. He'd come by and check out my stock from time to time. We'd have a good yarn, he'd take me out to dinner at the pub, and sometimes he'd kip the night. Of course, Jim's night parrot came up. Orcherton had heard rumours and was keen to know more. Once he realised I was getting titbits from Jim, he was very interested. We had a few beers one night, and he offered to pay for any information I could give him."

"He wanted to buy intelligence on Elder?"

Flanagan grimaced. "Yes. And I agreed. I mean, I needed the money. And it seemed harmless ..."

"Yes, of course. But you repeated everything Elder told you to Orcherton? For how long?"

"About the past two, maybe three years. He said he just wanted to give Jim a run for his money, a bit of competition. I never thought it would lead to ..." He swallowed.

"We don't know who murdered Jim Elder, Mr Flanagan, so there's no need to blame yourself. Besides which, you haven't done anything wrong."

"That's what I keep telling myself."

"How much did Orcherton know about Elder's movements?"

"Not where he was going, except roughly. Somewhere in the far southwest of the state. But he knew when he was leaving on trips, and roughly what route he was taking. I got the feeling he was planning to follow Jim, find out where he was going."

"Did he?"

"I honestly don't know. He never told me much about what he was actually doing. He'd always fob my questions off, say it was just a game."

"Where is Mr. Orcherton based?"

Flanagan looked puzzled. "I have no idea. He's one of those guys who just talks but never tells you anything. I don't know where he lives."

"But you have a phone number for him?"

"No. He would always just ... get in touch. I asked

him for his number, and he said, 'Don't worry, I'll call you.' I never thought too much about it. Now I feel dumb."

"Mr Flanagan, none of this is your fault, but is there anything you can tell me about him? What does he look like?"

"Nothing special. About my height, average I suppose. A bit overweight. Maybe sixty, greying hair. A beard—sometimes."

"What kind of car did he drive?"

"He always turned up in a hire car, said he was just in the area for a few days."

Petersen gathered what details she could of Orcherton's appearance and the timing of his comings and goings over the past few years. This man was adept at covering his tracks. She would search his name on the system back at the office, but she already knew the prospects of finding more about him were limited.

She was almost ready to leave when she remembered another question for Flanagan.

"How well do you know a Dr Col Stringer?"

Flanagan looked blank. "Who?"

"Dr Col Stringer. I take it he's also involved in the bird trade."

Flanagan frowned, shook his head. "Sorry—I don't know that name."

Chapter 18

The community was a collection of small, weather-beaten houses improbably hidden in the flatness of the black soil plain. Jake swung their vehicle down a dusty lane lined with cars that had rusted beneath years of ever hotter summers. He slowed down when a wiry arm reached up from an old, time-worn sofa moored under a shadeless tree.

"Granddad," smiled Jake.

"Looks like he was expecting you."

"He would be."

"Did you let him know we were coming?"

"Nope," laughed Jake in a high-pitched whinny, the happiest sound Butler had heard him make.

"'Bout time you came to see us," croaked the old man as they pulled up next to him. "In bloody trouble, as usual."

"It's my doing, this time," apologised Butler.

"I doubt that," said Granddad. "That boy's been gettin' in scrapes since he was a nipper."

A slender woman with black, shining eyes and

wearing a bright dress opened the screen door.

"Give your mother a hug, and don't stay away so long again, Jake Varoy. Why didn't you phone?"

"Mum, it has been too long, I know," said Jake, stepping out of the truck and striding up to her.

She seized him in a fierce embrace. She beamed at Butler. "This must be your mate, Queensland's most wanted, eh? He looks harmless to me," she laughed.

"Yeah, Mum, this is Ric. He's a friend."

Butler was touched by the proud affection in Jake's voice. He offered his hand. "Nice to meet you, Mrs Varoy."

"Call me Karen, love. And I don't do handshakes." She put her arms around him. "Thanks for bringing him home."

"It's my fault he couldn't phone you," said Butler. "I broke his phone."

"It was an accident," said Jake, winking at Butler. "Where's Dad?"

"Inside, making breakfast for you boys."

"Breakfast?" asked Granddad. "Can I have mine out here?"

"Nice try, old man," answered Karen. "You've already had yours, Varoy. And you're getting too fat anyway. I'll bring you a cup of tea." She winked at Butler. "He'll probably die in that chair. Can't get him out from under that tree."

Butler followed the old man's gaze and peered through a web of bare branches tipped with red flowers. Warm thoughts of his mother reminded him just how long it had been since he had been greeted with an embrace as welcoming as Karen's. He couldn't recall the last time he had felt so relaxed in the company of others—so at-home.

After a hearty breakfast of bread and fried sausages, Butler sat with Jake and his parents on the bench next to Granddad's sofa. A Woodswallow came and dipped its brush-tipped tongue deep into the red blossoms. Granddad stared through the branches at the sky.

Karen squeezed Jake's hand. "So, Ric, how much trouble are you boys in exactly?"

Butler saw where Jake had inherited his directness. "It's hard to say, Karen. I'm not sure what's happened since we left, but I have a feeling it will take a while to sort this out."

"Stay here as long as you want, Ric," said Jake's father. "Any friend of Jake's is welcome here."

"Thank you, Thad. But I really don't want to bring trouble here."

"Trouble!" Thad roared with laughter. "We're always in bloody trouble! We'd be on first-name terms with the coppers for a thousand miles around—if we actually liked the bastards." He shook his head with rueful amusement. "But seriously, we can look after you, no worries."

"Yeah, we'll be okay, Ric," said Jake. "The cops will turn up sooner or later, but they won't find us here. We have a good spot we can go, out of harm's way. Eh, Granddad?"

"You're taking me with you, boy," replied Granddad, as if he already had it planned.

"I see you watching those birds, Ric," said Thad. "You a birdwatcher, eh?"

"Yeah, I'm partial——"

"That's not the half of it, Dad," interrupted Jake. "It's a bird that got us into this trouble!"

"Oh?" Thad grew wide-eyed.

"Yeah, that night parrot they've been making such a fuss about in Brisbane. Ric's been ... what would you say ... following it up. And someone's not happy about it."

"Why would that be?" asked Thad.

"I wish I knew, Thad. I wish I knew," said Butler.

"Here she is," cried Jake. "My little cousin."

A skinny, young woman walked towards them, waving happily as Jake called to her. Butler squinted. Surely he could not have met her before, but she cut a familiar figure. As the contours of her face came clearer, he stared harder until he had to look down, red-faced. He gathered his cup clumsily and made to turn away.

"I think Ric's partial to that kind of bird," chuckled the old man. "Comes from good stock that one; her grandfather was popular hereabouts, with the birds, if you know what I mean. Spread himself pretty thin, the old bugger."

Karen playfully swiped at the old man and got up, winking again at Butler. "You're the only old bugger round here, Varoy."

Chapter 19

A sliver of daylight shone through Petersen's office window and cut across the papers on her desk. In silence, without the constant whir of office machines, she probed the documents laid out in front of her hoping the morning light would lay everything bare.

"Good Morning," said Nick Laurance as he strolled into Cairns CIB. "You look wrecked, have you been here all night?"

Petersen rested her forehead in her hand. "Feels like it," she said, looking up from eyes a little pinker than usual. "I wasn't sleeping well, so I came in early."

Laurance dropped his bag by his desk and looked her over again. His eyes showed genuine concern.

"What's bothering you, Eileen?"

She leaned back in her chair, uncertain how much to confide. Laurance had always been more than friendly to her and, despite his no-nonsense work approach, a good listener.

"It's this Elder case. It has too many loose ends. I can't get a grip on it."

Laurance pulled up a chair and sat opposite her. "Based on the briefings, I'd say the simplest explanation is the right one. Butler was at Elder's house on the day of the murder and immediately after went on the run. Not the actions of someone with nothing to hide. I don't know what the young bloke's involvement is, if that's what you mean by a loose end."

"Butler doesn't fit the profile of a murderer," said Petersen, lightly shaking her head. "I'd almost swear it couldn't have been him. Passionate, yes, but a murderer—it doesn't fit."

"Why, because he's a calm, friendly, and well-spoken citizen? A lot of criminals slip through first interviews because they seemed *nice*." In the air, Laurance drew inverted commas with his fingers. "Anyone can become a killer in the right circumstances—it could have been an accident or a disagreement that got out of control."

Petersen sensed Laurance prickling a little. Did he disapprove of her trusting her instincts or had he sensed she liked Ric Butler? Absurd, she had only met him once. But there was an openness in Butler's steady gaze that warmed her. She hoped her judgement of him was right.

Nick Laurance had, in various ways, hung his heart on his sleeve for her from the moment she'd arrived in Cairns. He was the only cop who appreciated her for her intelligence and hard work. And the only man in the office who called her by her first name. Although she respected him, a romance with a superior officer was never going to be a good idea. Since the Christmas party, where he had gained enough Dutch courage to ask her out and she had had the good sense to decline, he hadn't broached the subject of romance again. But any inkling of interest in another man sparked tacit disapproval from him. That he could be possessive about her rankled.

Laurance stared at her. "Apart from the young bloke involved, what are the other loose ends?"

"There's no motive. No evidence that Butler had ever even met Elder prior to that day."

Laurance tut-tutted. "Absence of evidence is not evidence of absence, Eileen. Suppose Butler is a smart guy who knows how to keep a low profile? According to Prescott from AFP, Butler is suspected of being involved in wildlife trading. If that's true, it's almost certain the two knew each other."

"Prescott's testimony doesn't sit well with me. There is no concrete evidence linking Butler to smuggling. Quite the contrary, he's been battling against it for years."

"And receiving no recognition. Overlooked for promotion, unpopular with his co-workers ..."

"According to whom?"

"His boss. If you believe your own report."

"Okay, but his boss is a ... seems biased against Butler, and has implicated him on very skimpy evidence."

"What about the airport fiasco? Why didn't he ask for backup to apprehend the perps? I'm just saying, based on his lacklustre employment report, Butler might be considering early retirement options."

"I can't explain Butler's behaviour at the airport, but——"

"And we know Elder was known to Butler because he attended Elder's night parrot presentation. Doesn't it seem odd that he went to Brisbane at his own expense, claiming to be sick after his boss refused him permission to go?"

"Every wildlife enthusiast is interested in the night parrot, Nick."

Laurance paused. Petersen could almost hear the cogs turning in his head.

"There are a couple more persons of interest, Nick."

"Oh? Who are they?"

"Well, it's tricky. Dr Col Stringer, a former Queensland Museum researcher who dropped out of sight years ago is suspected of illegal wildlife trafficking. He was in recent contact with Elder."

"How do you know that?"

"James Marsh had this photo of Stringer." She held up her phone to show Laurance the image she had snapped at Marsh's house. "Marsh didn't like Stringer; said he was secretive in his dealings with Elder. And if keeping a low profile makes you a suspect, Stringer is a prime candidate. I can't find any leads on him at all."

"Who else?"

"Dick Orcherton, an even more mysterious bird collector and dealer, obsessed with Elder and the night parrot. He paid for information on Elder's movements. But I can't find any leads on him either. You have to try hard to be as invisible as this guy. I've approached every contact I've got in the avicultural industry, and nobody has heard of him."

"You've been busy, Eileen. But short of solid leads wouldn't you say?"

"Agreed. And we have about as much chance of learning of Butler's whereabouts as the other two."

"Perhaps not."

"What do you mean?"

"Weagle phoned me on my way here. He has tracked Butler's phone to Lockhart River on the Cape. Now there's a haunt of wildlife smugglers if ever there was one."

Chapter 20

Butler sat on the ground, just out of sight of the houses, watching the plain. Something out there spoke to him, offering him protection. It was a fragile, sandy awareness resurfacing from his boyhood when he gazed into the same big sky that stretched in every direction to the horizon. In the flatness below, the breeze brushed through tufts of grass dappled with golden afternoon light. A mosaic of pebbles, lizard scales, and seed pods directed warmth into the soles of his bare feet, and the dry heat against his skin transported him to an untroubled place.

A family of emus, a male with eight half-grown chicks, stared back at him. He waved his hat, an old bush trick he had learned as a kid, which enticed the father emu to venture closer, the necks of his playful offspring a wriggling anemone behind his back.

Butler was enjoying the comedy of the giant birds' curiosity. They were wild and free, able to roam the endless plain on a whim. He imagined staying here, sleeping under the stars and spending each day cloaked in sunshine. Maybe he could learn to track, to hunt ...

"Ric! There you are." Jake's voice boomed across the grass. The emus backed up.

Butler looked down at his feet, embarrassed at his fantasy. Jake strode purposefully towards him. "We need to get going. Go to that quiet spot."

"Already?"

"Yeah. The cops could show up anytime. Nobody will tell 'em we're around but we best get out of sight."

Butler's heart sank as the reality of his fugitive status engulfed him again.

"You'll like this place, Ric, it's Granddad's old spot, peaceful. We should go now. We don't want to bring troubles here. There's enough already."

"Yeah, of course. I'm sorry I got you into this mess."

"We'll work it out. In the meantime, we'll hear some of Granddad's old stories. You will, anyway. I can catch up on some sleep," he chuckled.

The Hilux was already packed up with provisions and blankets. Old Man Varoy got comfortable in the back seat, grinning to himself. Karen loaded Butler up with the bread she had baked that morning. Her face was resolute, but he could detect the concern settling into the creases around her eyes.

"Here's a phone," she said, handing it to Jake. "I borrowed it from your cousin. Just let us know you're okay when you get a chance."

Thad gave them a rifle, smiling gently at the alarm on Butler's face.

"In case you get a shot at a nice little roo—would be sweet with that rice."

"Ah, okay. Sounds good—thanks, Thad. For everything."

"Where you from, Ric?"

"I grew up in Brisbane, but lived out bush before that as a little kid. Somewhere out this way, I suppose—I can't remember. My mother never talked about where we came from. But it was flat, I remember that much. And the grass was yellow."

Thad looked at him curiously. "Maybe your family can help you work out where you're from, help find a connection."

"I wish I had family, Thad, but it was just me and Mum."

"That makes it harder, for sure, but there's always a way back home." Thad nodded his head towards the dozing body on the back seat. "Eh, Dad? You asleep, Dad?"

Old Man Varoy spoke without raising his eyes. "Always a way home, that's right."

The shadows grew longer as they drove from the black soil onto sandy country where low rises broke the flatness of the horizon, and the grass of the plains retreated into defiant clumps of spinifex. Jake motioned to the rear vision mirror with an affectionate grin. Glancing back, Butler saw the old man, nodding serenely in time with each bump along the track, his eyes lost dreamily in deep creases.

"He knows this country as well as a kangaroo does," whispered Jake.

Jake steered towards a rise where reddening light caught bright-lichened boulders. A startled bustard quickstepped away, its blue eyes rebuking them from its upraised head. As they pulled up alongside the rocks, Granddad called out. Butler knew this practice but had never heard it so eerily intoned. The old man's voice quavered, almost stammering, pitching from nasal to a high, ringing falsetto, as he soothed the spirits of this place with the old language. He jumped from the truck, looking twenty years sprightlier. As he disappeared into a gap between boulders, the dying echo of his song sank into the stone.

"We'll give him a minute," said Jake. "Let him get the house in order."

Butler turned to survey his surroundings, the unexpected panorama startling him. The rock pile, an eminence barely discernible on approach, commanded a vista more expansive than any he had seen in almost a thousand kilometres. Mitchell Grass country formed an ochre band across the eastern horizon until it chopped abruptly to the surrounding purple sands, spattered with bright straw-coloured dots.

Jake looked at Butler, raising his chin. "My country. Granddad brought me out here when I was small."

"Still bringin' you here, young 'un," came the old man's voice. "I have ways to show you, don't go thinking you're grown up yet."

Granddad stood at an opening in the rocks, beckoning them to follow. Jake gestured for Butler to go first. Plunging into the darkness, he was blinded until a sliver of cinnamon light silhouetted the old man.

The cavern's deceptively roomy interior opened into a cathedral-like chamber, the evening light reflecting onto the sandy floor from a high wind-polished rock face. The natural skylight illuminated smooth grotto walls striped with eons of colour and overlain with millennia of ochre and charcoal paintings. A blackened plume directly below the opening marked generations of fires, invisible to the outside.

"You are welcome here, Ric," said the old man. "This is where I grew up."

Jake entered the chamber carrying a bundle of kindling which Granddad began to arrange in the fireplace, plainly savouring the ageless ritual.

"You'll sleep well here," Jake assured Butler. "I always do. In fact, I'll have a lie-down right now in my old sleep spot." He ducked under the overhang furthest from the fire and melted into the shadow underneath. "If I don't wake up, just toss a blanket over me later, will you?"

The old man lit the fire and smiled triumphantly. He looked up, meeting Butler's eyes with a penetrating gaze. Unable to look away, Butler felt himself disarmed, as layer by layer peeled away without a word.

Feeling for once he needed no excuse, Butler strolled outside to watch the dying of the day. The plain, maroon, grew darker one grain at a time. Each shadowing minute the coolness on his skin drew him deeper into the landscape, pushing his old world further away.

"I saw you," said the old man, suddenly next to

him. "How you looked at that girl—like you knew her."

"She ... she reminded me of someone."

"You remind me of someone." The old man watched the changing colours too. "And you—you're looking for someone."

"I am looking, Uncle, it's true; but maybe for my place, not someone. I don't know if there is anyone, any family for me."

The old man shrugged. "Same thing; place, family. You find one, you got the other."

"I stared at that girl because she looked so much like my mother. I came here to hide from something, but ever since I got here, I feel ... exposed. Like I've arrived at the place I was headed, not just this last few days but for a long time. Maybe Jake told you, about me, my name and all——"

"No, he didn't. But I see who you are. And I see your mother—just like that girl. I know who she was. Not from here, but I know her. And I know who you are. Your old man, he was a cousin. Lot of his lot round here."

"My father was from here?"

"Not here, but we know all of his lot, a long way 'round here. Plenty of them."

Butler's mind rebelled against the improbability he could have ended up here by sheer coincidence. But then, two days ago, he had no idea he might be indigenous, never even contemplating that possibility. Even after Jake's tirade, his conscious mind could not latch onto the idea. But as soon as he saw the girl, he knew. The red-flowering tree, his mother's voice, the colour of his own eyes, it all fell into place.

"You and me are the same boy," said Granddad. "Hidden away, so we couldn't be taken away. My granddad brought me here where nobody could find me. Nobody could check my skin. Same reason your mother took you away."

The secret his mother had kept for so long swept through him as sudden as a summer storm, his teenage anger coming back to sting him like hail in the face. All those years she pretended the past didn't exist, and for one reason; to protect him. During his later years he could have worked it out, if he'd had the courage. But he kept the secret for her, long after she'd gone ...

He looked self-consciously over at the white beard catching the last of the light. The old man's face, gleaming dimly, might have been looking in any direction. He shared a sublime oneness with the landscape, as though he would melt into the rocky ground if Butler looked away. Butler yearned for that sense of belonging and recognised now it was entirely missing from his life.

"Sorry, Uncle," he said, without thinking.

"Don't you be sorry, boy. It's hard, I understand that, you know I do. But you came here for a reason. You might have thought it was just an accident, coming here. Maybe you thought you were just looking for that bird—and he's here too—but no accident. You had to come here—to find your way."

"That's how it feels, Uncle, as if I was pulled here. I didn't want to come, but I had to. My mother's family, there are still some here?"

"Near here, we can show you. Your father's people too. Plenty of them."

"Butlers?"

"Butlers, no, that's your mother's mob."

"But why would she tell me——?" Butler stopped abruptly. He was treading water in a tangle of emotions, kicking hard to stay in one place. "Wait a minute, Uncle. Did you say the bird is here?"

"That green one that spends his days hiding in the porcupine grass. Yeah, I know him."

"You've seen it, Uncle?"

"Since I was a nipper when we used to chase it out of the grass. He's not always here; comes and goes. We know when he's around cos we hear him in the night."

"What does it sound like?"

"Ehm, not like those other parrots, not screechy. More like this—" He wet his lips, then blew a delicate, tinkling whistle. He winked at Butler as his whistle swelled to a slight crescendo, before dropping away, only to be repeated a second time but a note lower.

Despite his many nights in the bush, Butler had never heard a sound like it. It reminded him of something, a cuckoo perhaps, but not quite the same.

"You're right, it's different from the other parrots. Maybe a little like a ground parrot, from the coast."

"Never been there. But that's the sound. He's still here, sometimes."

"You still hear them here?"

"Haven't been out here for a long while now. But a few years ago he was here. Not so many anymore, but sometimes. I'm guessing he'll be here now," said the old man, softly. His gaze shifted to his broad, dusty feet.

"Is something wrong, Uncle?"

"My granddad knew about him, why he comes and goes like the rain, and why he's out in the dark, not like the other parrots. But he never got to tell me the story before he died. There's nobody left I can ask now."

Butler felt the ache of grieving in the old man's voice. The ancient story was as lost as the parrot, as lost as Butler himself was, all swamped by the same tide of change that had swept the landscape. His mother was swept away with it, and without her he felt as if he was drowning. Could he really find answers here? His rational mind chided him for allowing emotion to cloud his judgement; everything the old man had said seemed questionable. It was, after all, sheer chance he had come here, to the home of someone he had only met last week. There was no rhyme or reason to it, just desperation.

"If you believe in magic, Ricky," his mother had whispered one night as she tucked him into bed, "you'll have magic."

She had believed. But magic didn't happen for her. She hated living in the city. Although she never spoke about the bush, these vast open plains must have been what she dreamed of, especially when she drank in the daytime, and slept on the couch with that crooked smile on her pretty face.

I'm an idiot for believing magic could suddenly start happening to me, Butler thought to himself.

Chapter 21

After a long, fruitless morning in the office, Petersen's attempt at an afternoon nap was shattered by the strident lorikeets gathering in the fig tree behind her house. It was a twilight show she enjoyed, often with a small glass of Chablis on the weekend, but she had never tried to sleep through it before. Now, with her senses jarred back to alertness, she could not ignore the hypotheses generated by the relentless mental sifting in her head. She reached for her mobile and brought up the photo of Stringer.

"Who the hell are you?" she whispered.

He was an undistinguished-looking man, and her hunch was possibly nonsensical, but leaving stones unturned was not her style. She emailed the photo to Graham Flanagan and her list of bird breeders and dealers. It was anybody's guess how long she'd have to wait before she heard from Flanagan. Even the mention of him carrying a mobile phone brought on a near panic attack. She hoped another breeder would recognise Stringer although, with her own investigative net exhausted, it seemed a long shot.

Could Orcherton and Stringer be working together? If she couldn't make inroads into their involvement, all roads still led to Ric Butler, and her intuition told her he wasn't their man. She was equally certain someone was surreptitiously moulding a conspiracy against Butler. But why? The entire case stank like a dead rat under the floorboards.

Chapter 22

Butler woke in the darkness after the last of the day's heat had drained from the rocks and the cave felt icy. He pulled his blanket tighter, realising Jake had been right; he had slept soundly, even after the confusion of Granddad's fancies. The breathing of another person drifted from his left, Jake in his burrow. The fire still glowed; the old man must have stoked it during the night, but the orange embers struggled to penetrate the wintry air. He looked in that direction but could see only the coals. Maybe Granddad was listening silently too.

A distant birdcall sounded; dawn must be closer than he thought. It seemed odd that a bird would sing on such a cold night, beneath a still black sky. The call was a single, low whistle he couldn't place. Minutes passed and it sounded again; this time he heard a second, lower note. The song came again, a little stronger, as if a breeze had caught it. The sound, although a long way off, sounded uncannily like the birdcall the old man had made at sunset. He ought to look, not that he had any chance of finding the source with only his Maglite. He sat up and turned on the torch with his hand cupped over it. Shining the dim light towards the fire, he saw Granddad was gone. No wonder the sound was identical. The silly old bugger was out there in the dark, probably poking around clumps of spinifex searching for a ghost.

He laughed ruefully, backing down into the warmth of his blanket. The sound had stopped and no doubt the old man would come tumbling back into the cave to warm up. Just as he was dozing off, he stiffened as another sound carried into the cave. It was so distant he wasn't sure he had really heard it; the unmistakable cough of a Toyota starting up.

"Jake!"

Jake mumbled a groggy reply then, registering the urgency in Butler's voice, threw his blanket aside and switched on his torch.

"Your granddad's taken the truck."

Running from the cave, Jake's torch light beamed against the cabin of their stationary Hilux. Confused, Butler squatted on the ground to scan a black skyline, barely discernible in the east. Nothing broke the flatness. A flashing light caught his peripheral vision and his head whipped to the north. Gone again. It had to be the old man, with a torch.

"Ric, what's going on? Where's Granddad?"

Butler pointed his torch in the direction he'd seen a flash. "I think he's over there. I saw a light."

"That doesn't sound like him ... he's never used a torch, the silly old coot."

"I'm sure I heard a vehicle. Who else would be out there?"

"Nobody. Come on, let's find him."

Dawn's early light crept dimly over the spinifex, the bleached flower heads pale against the dark earth.

"Let's split up, Ric, we can cover more ground. I'll stay within sight of your torch."

"Okay, yell if you need me."

In the slowly growing twilight, Butler strained to see a dark termite mound that split the horizon up ahead. The illusion was shattered when a snaky form rose from it.

"Uncle?" he called.

"I heard him," whispered the old man, sitting with his arm raised. "That bird. He's here."

Butler held his breath. He squinted but could see nothing but tufts of spinifex. Could his night parrot really be out here?

Jake's torch light swung towards them.

"Granddad! What the hell are you doing strolling around out here?"

"I heard Ric's parrot."

"Wasn't it you making the parrot call?" asked Butler.

"Not me, no. It was two parrots singing. One sang for a long time, and another joined in afterward. They went quiet when the Toyota started up."

"I knew I hadn't imagined the truck. Where is it?"

"Headlights went that way." Granddad pointed north over miles of flat desert country, endless undulations of gravel, and three-foot high hummocks of spinifex.

"Who the hell would be out here?" asked Jake. "The years we've been coming here, we've seen no one. Not even the station owner grazes stock out this way."

The old man cocked his eyebrows. "Two strange fellas out here a summer ago. They were searching for something."

"How long did they hang around?" asked Butler.

"A few days. They were poking their noses into the spinifex. Then at night, they'd sit silently in the darkness, like they were waiting for something."

"How do you know they weren't talking?" asked Jake, an amused expression on his face.

"I snuck out of my cave and crept up on 'em like a snake," said Granddad. "Ha. They never even knew I was there. Strange fellas too. And always the same two."

"Was it them tonight?" asked Butler.

"Nope. The one I heard sounded different and he was real worked up about something."

Butler and Jake stared at each other and spoke in unison. "Not a chance ..." they said.

"Maybe they were mining prospectors," ventured Butler. "Where was the truck parked, Uncle?"

As the grey light gained colour, the old man walked to where the Toyota had started up. A few hundred metres ahead, a ray of sunlight glinted off something.

"Looks like some kind of surveying equipment ..." began Butler, stopping mid-sentence when he saw the arc of more poles.

"Bloody hell, it's a mist-net setup!"

He ran towards a bird caught in the far end of the net.

"Ric, we need to disappear before they get back. We can't have anyone finding this cave, or us for that matter. Chances are they've seen the news."

Butler kneeled by the net. "I don't believe this. These birds are dead. What the hell is going on?"

He pawed at the net, untangling the stiff body of an orange chat. "They're dried out! Who the hell would leave them here to die?" His chin trembled like a young child's. He gently untangled the second bird from the net, its flame-coloured feathers still so vital. "There's something wrong here. I'm waiting here until this bastard gets back, then I'll give him a lesson to remember."

"He's not coming back," said Jake, holding up another section of net. "He got what he wanted. Here, have a look."

A clump of feathers revealed where another bird had been caught.

"He took this one out," said Jake.

Time froze as Butler stared down at the feathers and was transported back to the slideshow in Brisbane. Brilliant green feathers darkly patterned. Blood began to pound violently in his temples and his legs felt weak.

"Ric, are you okay? You're shaking." Jake grabbed Butler by the shoulders as his trembling legs buckled underneath him.

"We have to get after him," Butler stuttered. "The bastard's taken a night parrot!"

"Oh shit! He's a good half hour ahead of us and we don't know where he's gone!"

Butler straightened, staring at Jake with startling

intensity. "Think Jake! Where's he heading?"

"Damn it, let me think. The road to Jundah—it's the quickest way out of here."

"Quick, help me get these nets down."

"What about Granddad? We can't take him with us, Christ knows where we'll end up," said Jake.

"I'm not going anywhere with you fellas," said Granddad holding up one of the dark green feathers. "Thaddeus will be here with my bread tomorrow."

"Are you sure, Granddad?"

"Just get that bird and bring him back to his country," he commanded with an accusing scowl at each of them. "Go on!"

Chapter 23

The Hilux raced into Jundah as the place was coming to life. Butler, his heart thumping from the breathless drive, surveyed the street with horror. "Shit! How are we going to find him?" Of the twenty cars in the street, every last one was a Toyota.

Jake's usual calm morphed into a tornado. "We're looking for Stringer, right?"

"I don't know, mate. I'm not sure of anything right now."

"Look, I'll take this side of the street, you go up that side. If he's here, we'll spot him."

Butler's brittle nerves jangled as he made his way along the footpath. He scanned the back of utes filled with cages, sacks, and boxes, trying to slow his thoughts into something his brain could cope with. Three times he heard a Toyota leap into life. Three times he glared at a cowboy-hatted local, one of them— the town realtor—fixed him with a homophobic stare. He dropped, flat-arsed, onto the kerb. Only yesterday the desert had been his sanctuary, now it was a hostile foreign land.

Jake half-ran across the street. "Ric, what have you found? Anything?"

Butler shook his head.

"Damn! What now?"

"I don't know. We have no clue where he's heading, or if he even came this way."

"He had to have come this way, it's the quickest way out of here."

"We're just guessing! We're in a cat and mouse game forgetting there's an even bigger cat chasing us." Butler picked up the phone. "Maybe it's time we handed ourselves in."

"No way!" said Jake. "You won't get a signal out here anyway."

Butler's eyes looked more defeated than Jake had seen them, even on that last evening before Palladia. He shook his head without conviction.

"Ric—we're not giving up on this! Ric?"

"I'm going to check my messages." He started towards the public phone. "I'll be back in a minute."

Given the events of the past few days, Butler expected a few messages. He was taken aback when the robotic voice announced he had thirty-eight. As he watched Jake wander along the street kicking stones with his dust-covered boots, a pleasant female voice spoke to him.

"Mr Butler ... er, Ric ... it's Senior ... Eileen Petersen. Professionally, I must insist you come into the station to assist with our enquiries. Personally, I don't understand why you've disappeared, but I think I have some idea after speaking with your boss. I need to know if you have any information on Dick Orcherton, the bird dealer. Please call me on this private number. Thank you, take care. Bye."

Butler replayed the message. She hadn't taken long to smoke out Weagle. Perhaps she could help him. He could trust her, he felt sure of it. But there was no way he was walking into a police station. He leaned out of the booth and scanned the roadside for Jake.

Butler listened to two more messages, when a frantic Jake came sprinting towards him with arms waving.

"Ric, we have to move, I know which way he went!"

"Are you sure? What happened?"

"Come on! He's an hour ahead of us at least."

Butler slammed the cab door shut as the Toyota skidded backwards, throwing up a spray of gravel. "How did you get onto him?"

"Bush telegraph, Ric," beamed Jake, pointing at a group of women sitting under the shade of a rock fig. Their three heads slowly turned as Jake sped clear of the town's last building.

"They saw a fat bloke with a beard come through this morning. It fits, Ric. He wasn't a local, and he was driving a white Landcruiser ute."

"Where's he headed?"

"North. He's headed north."

Over the years, Butler had had plenty of reason to speculate which routes were the quickest way out of Queensland. North would have been his choice too. Every one-horse town had a mini airstrip; places where a smuggler could disappear easily, places short on government officials where nobody would care too much about a parrot.

Butler switched on the radio as the hour rolled over. His thoughts shifted back to the other two phone messages he'd retrieved. The first, Boy asking him to get in contact urgently because he suspected the *kumander* could be in Australia; and the second, Bob with more information on Stringer. Everything was happening at once, but the phantom they were chasing seemed as invisible as the night parrot.

Jake turned up the volume.

"... Police are following strong leads on the whereabouts of the two perpetrators wanted in connection with Jim Elder's murder." Jake swiped at the radio. "Where do they get this stuff? Leads my arse!"

Butler chuckled. "It might have something to do with me dumping my mobile phone in a semi-trailer."

"How does that give them a lead?"

"Well, I figured they'd track my phone, so when we stopped in Mount Molloy I threw it into a cattle carrier heading up the Cape."

Jake's eyes lit up as he pictured the phone heading northwards. "You're a bloody genius!" He cackled with delight.

Butler chuckled too but abruptly stopped. "I hope we're not headed straight into the arms of the bloody police."

"We'll find out soon enough." Jake put his foot down as the road opened up across a stony plain.

Butler scanned the horizon ahead. "I'll hunt you down like the vermin you are," he whispered.

Chapter 24

It was sunset when Petersen arrived home after another fruitless day at the office. There was still no word about Stringer's photo from Flanagan, who evidently didn't believe in answering his phone. She was freshly showered and had settled in a comfortable chair to watch the flying foxes cruising the backyard fig before she noticed the text message. The caller ID read 'private number', but the instant she saw the message began with her first name she knew who it was.

"Eileen, thanks for your message. No idea who Orcherton is, sorry. Will help any way and when I can. Ric."

He sounded safe, but preoccupied. She wondered where he was and whose phone he was using—Jake Varoy's, she guessed. She started to reread the message, when a bleep from the computer announced an incoming email. Brett Venables. He didn't keep birds, but had been included in her avicultural contacts because he seemed to be connected to everybody else on the list.

"Hello Senior Constable Petersen, I can't be of much help, as I don't know his name, however I have seen this man before. It was some years ago (maybe ten), and he was at the general aviation terminal here in Cairns waiting for the same small plane as myself, a freight service of sorts from Cape York. He seemed to know the pilot quite well, so perhaps the latter can identify him. The pilot is still in the area, his name is Aaron Wrench. I believe he still operates a package service, maybe under his own name (not sure). I should mention that although I have no proof, I believe Wrench may be suspect, in relation to illegal wildlife and possibly other dealing. Call me for further information if you like, 0410810427, Brett"

How could Venables, who seemed to know almost everyone in north Queensland and possess a near-legendary omniscience, come up blank on Col Stringer's name?

Still, Venables had given her a lead on Stringer. She grabbed her notebook and reread the message again. She had a gut feeling she could trust Venables. Despite him being investigated a year earlier in relation to a fauna smuggling operation, she had found him to be open and of a gentle demeanour. She wrestled the yellow pages directory from under a mound of office files and found Wrench's name. As feared, she reached his voicemail. "Wrench here. I'm in the air. Leave a message."

Wrench's voice held a hint of a North American accent, eroded by many years in Australia, but it was the gravelly disdainful tone that gave Petersen an unfavourable first impression. She put down the phone and changed back into her uniform.

She drove past several darkened terminal buildings before reaching the airfield's brightly lit security office. A beer-bellied man with an unlit cigarette dangling from his mouth walked to her car window. She relaxed when he smiled warmly.

"Hello, Miss. How can I help you?"

"Hello, I'm Senior Constable Petersen from CIB."

"Pardon me, Senior Constable." He quickly removed the cigarette and adjusted his sagging pants. "Ron Coleman."

Petersen guessed he was ex-military or former police. "Mr Coleman, I need some information on a tenant—Aaron Wrench—who runs a freight service."

"Come in, please. I'll get his details." Coleman, belying his looks, turned out to be meticulous in his record keeping and looked very much at home in an office. "Here we are—he lives in space forty-five, or rather his aircraft does. A Cessna 172." He pointed towards a row of planes. "Ah, that's his spot there, the empty one. He must be off on a run."

"Can you tell me where he's gone, and for how long?"

"Sure. I'll pull up the flight plan."

After a minute of clicking and scrolling through his database, Coleman looked perplexed. "Well, he hasn't cancelled his SAR. Probably means nothing, they forget all the time, the buggers."

"Sorry, what does that mean?"

"SAR—Search and Rescue. Anyone departing

a major terminal like this one has to lodge a SAR notification, which is cancelled once they land at their intended destination. Once landed, there is no need to mount a search and rescue operation. His last lodged flight plan was this afternoon, to Lockhart River. But as he hasn't cancelled his SAR, we don't actually know where he is."

"Lockhart River—that's Iron Range, yes?"

"Correct."

"Thank you, Mr Coleman. You've been very helpful."

"It's a pleasure to help a fellow law enforcer. I used to be in the police myself."

Petersen started to answer when she was interrupted by her phone. Finally, the call she'd been waiting for. She nodded and waved goodbye to Coleman.

"Hello, Mr Flanagan."

"Oh, how did you know it was me?"

"I have your number saved on my phone."

"I see. Does that mean I'm a person of interest?"

"Um, no, Mr Flanagan. Just a contact."

"Okay, good. Just a contact then. Because like you said, I've done nothing wrong."

After a pause, she realised he was waiting for something. "Um, Mr Flanagan?"

"Yes?"

"Why did you call me?"

"Oh, yes. To tell you, you sent me the wrong photo. You know, the picture you said was of Mr Stringer."

"I don't understand."

"Well, it's not Stringer."

"Why do you say that, Mr Flanagan?"

"Because it's Dick Orcherton."

Chapter 25

A cold breeze descended on Hughenden as the day died behind a leaden cloud bank. All day Butler had feared the scent was growing cold, but he forced himself to cruise the streets with hope. He and Jake had been lucky so far—regaining the smuggler's trail in Jundah—but without the help of the authorities they were forced to rely on guesswork and their gut instincts to keep heading north.

Butler felt exhausted. Every time he tried to rest, his thoughts turned to the plight of the bird; how terrified it would be, snatched from the open plains and confined to a box. He hoped the thief was experienced enough to care for it properly. Surely he must be. A night parrot was worth nothing dead.

Each time they had pulled into a small town, he had sensed Jake's growing frustration. Every place presented the same scenario—fuel attendants had seen no bearded man refuel, locals did not recall a stranger passing through, no unusual contents in the backs of utes—making their task seem more insurmountable than ever. They pulled over on Hughenden's main street and sat in silence. A small party of grey nomads cruised past them, looking for somewhere to eat.

"We're looking for the proverbial needle here," said Butler. "Are you sure you want to keep going?"

"We have to, Ric. We could be right behind him, and if we don't track the bastard down, he'll get away scot-free."

Butler smiled. Jake hung on like a bloody limpet on a rock.

"Okay, but we have to be more careful when we enter the towns. If you're seen with me—a wanted man—you'll go down. You should bail out while you can and I'll take my chances."

"Look, I'll be given a hard time no matter what I do. Besides, they're looking for us on Cape York."

Jake was right. Aiding and abetting was a serious crime, and he would pay for it. "Okay. I'm glad you're here, mate. Now we have to decide which direction to take."

"You reckon he's still heading north?"

Butler shrugged. "He can't risk getting that bird out of a major airport. He'll have to fly it out on a private plane."

"But how far could he get?"

"A small plane can get him to PNG or some Indonesian outpost where he can disappear pretty quickly."

"But the pilot? Aren't there security checks and customs clearances?"

"Not if the money is right."

The nomads reappeared, settling on the garishly-lit Chinese restaurant.

"We should eat too," said Butler. "We'll be able to think better with some food in us. I need to make some calls too."

"Okay, but I'm not giving up."

"He has to stop sometime, Jake. If he's not here, he's probably camping out of town in the dark."

"What if he's got long-range tanks and some food? Then he could drive through the night."

Butler tried to hide his feeling of increasing impotence. "Can you grab the takeaway, Jake? And leave your phone."

Jake looked at him with exaggerated dismay. "Country town Chinese—my favourite. Should I get a receipt for Weagle?"

Butler chuckled. Jake, who tried to keep a straight face, laughed too.

"Yeah. And make it large, eh?"

Butler filled the tank and jerrycans before the servo closed for the night, then got on the phone.

"Bob?"

"Ric! Man, it's good to hear you. I've left a ton of messages. I've been worried sick."

"Yeah, sorry, mate, I haven't checked my messages. You wouldn't believe the saga." Butler delivered a highly abridged version of the days' events.

"Bob? Bob, are you there?"

"Yes, I'm here. Dumbfounded, that's all. Where are you headed?"

"We'll keep heading north and hope we get lucky

again. He doesn't even know we're after him, so maybe we'll catch him unawares. I don't know Bob, but we can't give up now. We've chased this phantom halfway across bloody Queensland."

"Be careful, Ric. There're cops on the lookout for you on the Cape. You might run into a spot of bother if you keep heading that way."

"The Cape, you reckon? Remind me to explain that one to you later."

"Well, if you need an eye in the sky, I'm your man. I'm in Cairns. I was due for a fieldtrip anyway. I'll fly to Iron Range tomorrow morning."

"You can't, you crazy bugger! You'll find yourself in real hot water if you do."

"Only if I'm an accomplice. And for me to be an accomplice you would have to be a criminal. To hell with it! I'm going up."

"I owe you big time, mate. Listen, I have to make more calls, but you said you had some information on Stringer?"

"Oh, yeah. Seems he got sacked from the museum for his dodgy dealings, but the whole affair was hushed up because he had important connections—police and politicians, real white-shoe brigade stuff. Word is he was given a deal, but he had to relocate."

"Relocate? Where to?"

"No idea, mate, the information I got was vague."

Butler looked up to see Jake waiting patiently by the truck with two bags of Chinese. "Thanks Bob. It feels good to know you're up here. I have to go, but you can reach me on this number. Bye."

Butler knew he wouldn't be able to eat until he'd made one more important call. But how much could he tell Petersen?

He turned the caller ID off again and took a deep breath as the phone rang.

"Petersen here. Is that you, Ric?"

The warmth in her voice instantly comforted him.

"Yes, Eileen. Sorry to call so late——"

"No, it's fine. Where are you?"

"We think we could be following Stringer."

"Ric, if it is him, he could be dangerous. Leave it to the police."

"The bloody police are too busy looking for me. And anyway, whoever it is doesn't know we're following. But he used Elder's recording to catch a night parrot, so it's someone dangerous all right."

"What he's driving?"

"A white Landcruiser ute—heading north out of Hughenden. Not much to go on, sorry."

"And why do you think it's Stringer?"

"We got a description in Jundah; it sounds like him. Fat, beard, grey hair. We know he's been hanging around Elder. I'm not a betting man, but I'd put money on him."

"Right. I'll try to have him picked up. I'll distribute his photo and get a lookout order on him. Any idea where he's headed?"

"One of the small airstrips. He'll be keen to leave the country as soon as possible."

"Ric, one more thing. Stringer uses an alias—Dick

Orcherton. If you run across him, be careful. He sounds dangerous. He's certainly very clever."

"I have to save that bird, Eileen."

"Understood."

"Can you text me the photo of Stringer? I need to show somebody."

"I'll do it right away."

"Thanks, Eileen. Really. Okay, I have to go. Bye."

The smell of MSG-laden takeaway was never so welcome, filling the cabin of the ute as Jake climbed in. "They're authentic Chinese people in there, Ric. This tucker might be all right. Why are you smiling?"

"If Eileen Petersen believes half of what I said, Stringer might get picked up by the police."

"You spoke to the coppers?"

"Yep. And I told her what you told me. We're not stopping."

"Fine with me. But if Stringer's camped out, we could drive right past him. Maybe we should stop for the night. We can take our dinner out of town and find a quiet spot."

Butler looked at the darkness to the north of town, then nodded in agreement. "*Allons-y* then."

"What?"

"It's French for let's go."

Jake grinned slyly. "We might have been better off with the French than your lot."

Butler laughed. "I thought I was one of *your* lot."

Jake tilted his head to the north and snickered: "Allan Zee, mate."

Chapter 26

By the time Petersen had cleared her mind, it was well past the hour she would have normally phoned her boss. But events were moving so rapidly, she could no longer wait. The smuggler was heading north—with a night parrot no less—and Wrench was waiting at Cape York with a plane. If she didn't act fast, her lead was likely to vanish.

Laurance listened to her rapid-fire summary of the latest developments.

"Eileen, if this doesn't pan out, I'm going to look like a prize idiot. Is this information reliable? I don't suppose you will reveal your source?"

"I think you've already guessed, Nick. He's as reliable as I've got, and from what he said I'm almost certain this bird smuggler is trying to flee the country. Whoever he is, he's connected to the murder—he has Elder's night parrot recording. I have a description of him that sounds awfully like Col Stringer. And I have a good idea who the pilot is that's flying him out."

"How useful do you think a lookout order will be in

the bush with bugger all troops, Eileen? Bloody Butler and his mate are leading the Lockhart boys on a wild goose chase. I'd feel a lot happier if I had something concrete to give the Commissioner. Who's the pilot?"

"Aaron Wrench. He has a shady past, and he and his plane have dropped out of sight. Unusual for a licensed pilot to ignore protocol, don't you think?"

"You tell me, Eileen. But I admit, it doesn't sound good."

"Exactly, Nick. I need to get up there—up the Cape, fast."

Chapter 27

Camped out in thick cover, Butler tossed and turned, willing the eastern skyline to lighten so he and Jake could get moving. Time took on a different form when lying in the swag; each trickling minute used to reassure himself there was nothing more he could do right now to catch the king of thieves. He held Jake's phone above his head. Two bars. Why hadn't Boy responded to his message?

His thoughts turned to Eileen Petersen and what she might think of him. She probably had him figured for a lowlife because of the way he had manipulated her in the beginning. Those actions sat uncomfortably now. Despite her cool Scandinavian exterior, she had a warm heart. He needed to apologise to her. But that would have to wait until he had the bird.

Throughout his career he had thwarted hundreds of attempts to smuggle creatures out of the country, but the night parrot's abduction from its homeland struck like a hard blow to his gut. It belonged in the spinifex country; the place he had been taken from himself, the place his mother had to forsake to save his skin. The thought of the frightened bird alone in a cage, a thousand kilometres from those open plains, probably cold and hungry, was what kept him going.

Elder's murder had been the furthest thing from Butler's thoughts. But lying awake in the silent blackness, he thought of the larger-than-life bushman; so different from himself, yet they shared the same obsession. Just when the poor bugger had achieved legendary status, his love of the bird and his unwillingness to hand over the recording got him killed. An honourable end, in Butler's book. If Stringer was responsible, Butler prayed he got the punishment he deserved—if they could catch him. He was desperate to hit the road the moment dawn broke.

The phone vibrated in his hand.

"Boy?" he whispered. He glanced at Jake who never seemed to have a problem sleeping.

"Ric, that photo you sent me. Why do you want to know about him?"

"Stringer? I think he's a smuggler. *And* likely involved in murder."

"I've never heard that name. That's Bill Stocker, a British bird breeder based in Manila. He's been helpful to us for years."

As the picture burst into focus in Butler's mind, his worst fears were confirmed. The man they were chasing was a ruthless professional criminal.

"Don't tell me he's helped you apprehend smugglers?"

"How did you know?"

"Boy! He was eliminating the competition. It's him, the *kumander*," yelled Butler, startling Jake bolt upright. "And he's about to leave the country with a night parrot!"

"Damn me to hell, Ric! I can't believe I fell for it! Is he still in Australia?"

"We're hoping to pick up his trail at first light, but for all I know he could be in bloody Port Moresby by now."

"If he lands here, we'll pick him up."

"You'll be looking for him under three different aliases; Stocker, Dick Orcherton, and Col Stringer."

"Be careful, Ric. He's a dangerous man."

Butler ended the call, sinking back into the inky blackness.

"Ric, did you say Orcherton?" asked Jake.

"Sorry I woke you, Jake. Yes, another alias of Stringer's, it turns out."

"Shit! I didn't recognise him from the photo because of the beard, but it's the same guy, I'm sure."

"You've seen him before?"

"When I was a kid. He used to turn up out home and get some of the local men to help him trap birds. I didn't think anything of it at the time, but he must have been dealing way back then. We called him 'The Ork.' And get this, Ric ..." Jake nodded to himself with a wry smile. "Him and Weagle were thick as thieves."

Chapter 28

Petersen surveyed an endless woodland of Darwin stringybark as the rescue helicopter thudded Cape-wards. The last time she had been this far north—as a teenager—was when she accompanied her dad, an 'armchair' naturalist, who named the dominant trees of the landscape and each change of ecosystem for her. Her love of the bush was born on that trip.

After two hours in the air, a creek-side strip of gallery forest came into view, signalling the end of the Laura Basin. Flat brown plains yielded to the hilly forests of the McIlwraith, and finally the hazy outline of Mount Tozer. This was the Iron Range—the jungle of her imagination—an outpost of New Guinea in Australia.

The pilot gestured toward the airstrip which to her looked deserted. She cursed the delays they had encountered before leaving Cairns. For a time it seemed events conspired against her; first with the EMQ duty pilot sick, and then his replacement calling in at the last moment, struck down by the same Thai dump on Spence Street. It was a miracle she had found Ray

Leech, an old acquaintance from Townsville police—irreverent but reliable—who agreed to help.

When finally ready for a dawn departure, a pot-bellied figure had dashed awkwardly across the tarmac towards them. Coleman slumped against the bird, out of breath and wheezing.

"Sorry to hold you up, Senior Constable, but I've been thinking," he said, coughing violently. "Your father was a good man, one of the straight ones."

"You ran all the way out here to tell me that?"

"No, but I'm betting you're cut from the same cloth. You're after this fella, Stringer, right?"

"What makes you think that?" asked Petersen.

"I heard it on the grapevine. I'm ex-police. But what I didn't tell you was that I retired early because of what I call 'politics.'"

Petersen glanced at her watch. "I'm not sure I have time for this, Mr. Coleman?"

"Miss Petersen. I was bullied into early retirement by a senior police officer who didn't appreciate me exposing a gang of wildlife traffickers. Bullied is an understatement; my wife and my two young daughters were threatened."

"I'm very sorry to hear that, Mr Coleman. But I really don't have time for——"

Coleman cut her off mid-sentence. "Miss Petersen, you need to know the mongrel who held the noose around my neck was Karl Weagle!"

Weagle! His name hit her like a wave of stench. "Ray, get this bird in the air, and fast!"

As Leech lined up with the Iron Range runway

and descended for the landing strip, Petersen spotted a lone white Cessna parked on the tarmac. "Is that Wrench? We've got him."

"I wouldn't be so sure," said Leech, his eyesight evidently sharper than hers. "That's a Palm Cockatoo on the tail. Cape York Air, I think. The call sign is BKO. What are we looking for?"

"A Cessna 172. It has to be his."

"Whatever you say, Petersen. I'm dropping you by the strip manager's office."

She ran into the office. "Is that Aaron Wrench?" she yelled at a man half-buried under a mass of wiring.

"What the fuck is it now? Oh, sorry, Officer."

"Aaron Wrench! Is that his plane on the airstrip?"

"Nope. That's Bob Harrison's."

"Has Wrench been here?"

"Yep, took off half an hour ago. Why is everyone so interested in him lately?"

"What do you mean?"

"Harrison. The bird researcher. He asked where Wrench was going too."

"And where *was* he going?"

"Well, it was Atherton. But after one hell of an argument over the phone he switched to Bamaga."

"Where is Harrison?"

"In his plane."

Through the open door she heard the Cessna's engine revving.

The manager's radio crackled to life. "Bravo Kilo Oscar, Bravo Kilo Oscar, Cessna 172 departing Lockhart River for Violet Vale."

"Where the heck is Violet Vale?" snapped Petersen.

"An hour's flight south."

"But Bamaga is north. Isn't Wrench heading north?"

"That's what the man said."

There was time yet to stop Harrison taking off. Why was he interested in Wrench? But could she afford the delay? Wrench was heading for Bamaga, the last stop before Torres Strait. If she didn't catch up, he and Stringer would be gone. She sprinted back to the helicopter, deciding as she ran. "Bamaga, Ray! We have to go! Now!"

Chapter 29

The HF radio stuttered to life as the Hilux hugged another corner on the deeply corrugated gravel road heading north towards the Lynd.

"Ric?"

"Bob, where are you?"

"I just left Iron Range."

"Already? I thought—"

"This might sound crazy but I'm heading south on the scent of another plane. As I descended into Lockhart, I spotted another Cessna heading in the opposite direction—a commercial service belonging to Aaron Wrench, a dodgy bastard if ever there was one. Wrench told the strip manager he was headed to Bamaga, but he sure as hell wasn't headed that way when I saw him."

"Bob, you've lost me! What the hell is happening?"

"My guess is Wrench changed plans when the heat came down on him. Police arrived in a helicopter just as I left."

"Okay. We're almost at the Lynd, nearly off the dirt."

"Put your foot down, Ric, and check the airstrips close to the highway. Wrench didn't have time to refuel so he'll be looking to pick up Stringer, or whoever the hell you're chasing, from somewhere he thinks the police won't be waiting."

"We just passed the airstrip at Lyndhurst, but there are others at Conjuboy and Spring Creek. Shit, mate, there are dozens of airstrips out here."

"That's why I'm checking the northerly strips from the air. You just have to cover the southerly ones."

"You're a bloody genius, Bob!"

"Yeah. That's why I've got the Cessna and you're in a Toyota, mate."

Chapter 30

Leech aimed the helicopter for the tip of Australia; cruising low over dense forest and glittering mangroves towards the Coral Sea beaches. Petersen's quick search showed Bob Harrison seemed to check out; a bona fide and well-respected academic at UQ. His listed publications suggested he was a professional and ardent conservation biologist, surely not the type to be involved in wildlife smuggling—or was it a perfect cover? It was his profile picture that sealed her opinion of him. He had an honest face.

Wrench had to be crooked. No convictions or hard evidence, but Venables' opinion was good enough for her; and a Facebook photo she had seen of Wrench confirmed he looked as unfriendly as his voicemail message. But it was the man standing alongside him in the photo and the caption that made the hair on her neck stand: 'With my old pal Jim Elder—famous naturalist and discoverer of the legendary night parrot.'

Surely they would beat Stringer to Bamaga, even

if he had driven all night. Wrench would have to wait on the tarmac for him, giving her a chance to pick him up. She desperately hoped Stringer would be stopped at the Lakeland checkpoint, but the reality of a few policemen on the lookout in an area covering a hundred and twenty thousand square kilometres was hopeless.

Fifty metres below her, the white silica dunes of Shelburne Bay whizzed by. The colours and unspoiled beauty reminded her of the power of wilderness to bring her relief. When had she last taken even a few days off for herself? It was time, once this was over.

She wore her tiredness like a heavy cloak. Why had Wrench changed his flight plans? He couldn't know she was on to him. Closing her eyes, she tried to still her racing mind. Faces, places, photos, interviews, and her computer screen, all rang little bells. Her eyes popped open. Weagle! The bastard had found out she was tracking Wrench.

Wrench had been tipped off!

Chapter 31

A hundred and ten kilometres south-west of Cairns, Mount Garnet marked Butler's nervous arrival back into home territory. But with little more than a couple of pubs and a service station, he expected to be through it in a minute flat. By the time he spotted the checkpoint, it was too late to turn around.

"Shit ... we're finished now," said Jake.

"Steady," urged Butler, "just act natural. They're only checking the Cruisers."

A young policeman mechanically motioned their vehicle through.

"That was too close for comfort," said Jake. "Your police friend sure got things stirred up. I better drive and you lie low until we get through this area."

"You think they're not going to recognise your face?"

"You *are* joking, aren't you?" Jake laughed.

"You're right," said Butler, pulling over. "And we should take the old roads ... Oh crap! That's what Stringer's done; he's gone up through the old Petford road and dodged the bloody police."

"But how would he know there was a checkpoint?"

"I don't know, unless he's been tipped off. But those crappy roads will slow him down. We can reach Laura before him."

"Unless he's picked up by that plane before then."

Butler looked back at the impotent roadblock until his own efforts began to feel cruelly futile. "Do you think he's out there, Jake? It feels like we're chasing the bogeyman."

Jake looked back at him steadily. "Look at us. It's a bloody miracle we've made it this far with all the cops looking for us. Whoever's looking down on us will help us out." He cast his eyes upwards as he drove past the edge of town. "I just hope he didn't drive all night and get ahead of us."

"If he's taken the Petford way, we can cut him off on the Peninsula road. If we stay on the bitumen, we'll get there first."

Butler slumped in the passenger seat. "Those roads will be hard going on that poor bird."

Chapter 32

When Petersen landed on the Bamaga airstrip, it was empty.

"He's not here!"

"Doesn't look like anyone's been here," said Leech.

"Well, he can't go any further north than this, not if he wants to meet a car."

"Maybe he never came this way to begin with."

"If you were going to meet someone with an illicit cargo, where would you pick?"

"Some quiet station airstrip."

"And how would you leave the country?"

"Across the strait. But if he's already picked up his cargo, he won't have to stop here. He could carry enough fuel to make it to PNG, easy."

"He could be anywhere, couldn't he?"

"It's a needle in a haystack job, if you ask me."

Petersen's face flushed red. "I need to make some calls."

Chapter 33

The Hilux hummed along the bitumen, eating up the miles. Even with Jake driving, Butler's stare was glued to the road. He rubbed his eyes with his palms but couldn't shift the gritty fatigue that filled them. He jumped when the radio blasted to life.

"Ric, I've got him," yelled Bob. "Wrench's plane is on the old strip near Yalka."

"Are you sure it's him, Bob?"

"My oath, mate. I read his call sign with the binoculars."

"We're almost at Laura. How far away are we?"

"You're eighty kilometres from the turnoff. Then about ten k's to the strip."

"We don't know whether Stringer's ahead of us or still on the Petford road."

"I'll follow the main road towards you and see if I can spot him. If you see me overhead, you'll know he's behind you."

"What if you see him?"

"I'll double back to Yalka and land just as he gets

there. I don't want to land before that in case Wrench
tips him off."

    "But what if they're armed? You could get hurt!"

    "Well, you better put your foot down, mate!"

Chapter 34

Petersen was achieving nothing on this godforsaken airstrip. The few scheduled flights had arrived and departed earlier in the day, and the site manager had gone back to Bamaga. The strip was far enough from town, anyone could have landed undetected. Wrench could be long gone, or she might have missed him by minutes. The tarmac sent up a withering haze that licked at her flushed face. Her racing thoughts were interrupted by her ringtone.

"Ric?"

"Eileen!" He sounded panicked. "We need help. We know where Stringer is."

"Where are you?"

"Laura. He's either just ahead of us, less than an hour, or behind us on the Petford road."

"How do you know?"

"There's a plane waiting for him at the old Yalka airstrip. No time to——"

"Wrench! I've been looking for him all day. I'll

alert the police at the Lakeland checkpoint. They can head your way. Ric? Ric? Hello?"

She yelled to Leech who was checking his maps. "Ray, how long to get to Yalka Station?"

"Yalka? Where the hell is Yalka?"

"I don't know; maybe a hundred k's north of Laura."

"That's more than two hours away."

Petersen stamped on the tarmac and gritted her teeth, sheer frustration finally getting the better of her.

Chapter 35

The Hilux belted along the dirt road, the corrugations bouncing the gear in the back and clattering Butler's teeth. A plume of red dust trailed behind as he pushed the vehicle north as hard as he could. Every second counted now.

"The sign for Yalka," said Jake, pointing to the left. "Ric, slow down!"

"Sorry, Jake, I'm terrified Bob will meet them on the tarmac and try to tackle them himself."

"Okay, but let's just take this turn safely or we'll be no help."

"He must have spotted Stringer and gone back to the airstrip, otherwise we would have seen him long ago."

Jake clung hard to his seat as the Hilux spun around the corner, spraying gravel in its wake.

The badly surfaced road smoothed out as the Hilux hit its stride at ninety.

"Bloody diesel, come on," growled Butler.

"There's a plane," yelled Jake.

"Is it landing or taking off?"

"Wait ... it's landing. Yes, it's dropped below the horizon. It must be Bob."

"Go faster, you heap of shit," moaned Butler between gritted teeth.

"Hang on," said Jake. "He's taking off again. What the ...?"

The Hilux went airborne as they crested the final rise, landing in ankle-deep red dust that smothered the windscreen. "Shit! I can't see a thing," yelled Butler.

Jake hung his head out of the window. "There's a plane on the strip."

"That must be Bob. Wait for us, you bloody madman!"

The final two kilometres felt like a hundred as Butler pushed the Hilux to its limit, swerving wildly to avoid gaping potholes in the track. As soon as he saw the bare red surface of the strip, he swerved hard left, ploughing through knee-high anthills as he headed straight for the Cessna. He sped past the abandoned Landcruiser and screeched to a halt behind Bob's plane. Jake was already halfway out of the cab.

"Jake. Get in the right side and jump over into the back. Go!"

Jake could hear Butler running behind him as the figure in the cockpit waved frantically. Bob, wild-eyed, pulled Jake in through the door and shoved him into the back seat. Butler slammed the plane's door behind him. "Can we go after them?"

"Bloody Oath we can. This will be a rough take-off. Hang on!"

The propeller roared to life. The little cabin shuddered with every bump as the plane sped along the old runway. Finally, the rattling stopped as they soared into the air. Bob pulled a raking turn to the north and climbed abruptly. He and Butler looked at each other and breathed a sigh of relief.

"Welcome to Butler's flying circus," shouted Bob. He glanced over his shoulder. "Jake? Are you okay?"

Jake's face had turned white.

"You'll feel better in a minute, mate." Bob handed the binoculars to him. "Here, take these. See if you can pick them up and keep them in sight."

"You don't know how relieved I was to see you waiting on the tarmac," said Butler, putting his hand on Bob's shoulder. "I thought you'd be crazy enough to tackle them yourself."

"Nah, Ric. They were too quick for me. He was out of the Landcruiser like a jack-in-the-box. And Wrench ... he had the plane lined up ready to go. It was the fastest take-off I've ever seen. I was right behind him; even considered dropping in front of him."

Butler buried his head in his hands. "Sal would never have forgiven me, Bob."

"I saw her face, Ric. That's what stopped me."

"I see him!" yelled Jake. "Shit, they're a long way away."

"Only by two minutes. We'll be able to keep them in sight."

Butler could just make out the speck that was Wrench's plane. They had been so close behind their quarry and now they had to start the chase again. He gripped both sides of his seat fearing his frustration would soon turn to panic.

Bob glanced at Butler. "It's not over yet, Ric. We can follow him across the strait."

"Do we have enough fuel?"

"Yes, but Wrench has more. If he spotted my first flyby, he'll know I've been in the air for forty minutes longer."

"How far can they get?"

"They'll be able to reach the Trans-Fly, but not all the strips there have fuel."

"What if they land on a small strip and ditch the plane?" asked Jake.

"Then we'll have to ditch this one too," said Bob.

"Stop!" cried Butler, his eyes scrunched shut. "This is getting out of control. Now we're dumping *your* plane in the middle of a New Guinea swamp."

"Yeah, but we'll have *your* night parrot in our arms, Ric. And there's the matter of clearing both your names."

"But we don't know how crazy—or how desperate— these bastards are. If we follow them to New Guinea, and they're armed——"

"What about that copper friend of yours?" said Jake. "Petersen. Can't she help?"

"Petersen ... wait a minute—a tall blonde woman?" asked Bob. "The cop that got out of the chopper at Iron Range; I thought she was searching for Wrench. If they're still in the area, they might force him down."

"It's got to be her! I need to call her, but I've got no phone signal."

"We can try radioing through to Hann River," suggested Bob. "Archie can pass a message onto the police." He grimaced. "That's if he hears the radio—the bugger is usually pissed by lunchtime."

"He needs to get in touch with Senior Constable Eileen Petersen, in Cairns CIB."

"It's worth a try."

Chapter 36

Petersen didn't enjoy sitting still one bit. Especially not when there was a chase on. When the Lakeland police radioed her to say they'd found an abandoned Landcruiser ute and a Hilux at the old Yalka airstrip, she'd figured Wrench and his cargo had left there. The Hilux must be Butler's, but where had *he* gone? Was it possible he had been picked up by Harrison?

If Wrench had headed north, she might be able to intercept him.

"Ray, how long would it take a Cessna to get here from Yalka?"

"Just over two hours I reckon. Do you know when they left?"

"Up to an hour ago, by my calculations. Do you think you could force him to land if he comes this way?"

Leech laughed and shook his head. "You've been watching too many movies."

"I thought you were trained for that sort of thing."

Leech choked on his cigarette. "They train you to stay away from other aircrafts, not crash into them!"

Petersen suspected that Leech, despite his protests, was warming to the chase. Goodness knows, it had turned out to be the most action she'd seen on the force in years. Wrench must know Butler was chasing him by now. She pictured the two fugitives who—should they be able to cross the strait—could soon be standing on a tropical beach, smoking Cuban cigars.

"Have we got enough fuel to follow them across the strait?" asked Petersen.

"Yeah, but then what? We apprehend them on foreign soil and get speared by the good citizens for our trouble?"

"We need him to land in Australian territory. Do you have any suggestions?"

"Can we get on the radio and cut a deal with the pilot? I mean, bloody hell, how much can one bird be worth?"

"A couple of million dollars."

"What! Are you serious?"

"Plus, Stringer is a suspect in a murder investigation."

The Cairns dispatcher's number flashed on Petersen's phone. "Petersen here."

"Dispatch. Please call Archie at Hann River Roadhouse in relation to Ric Butler. Urgent."

Petersen scribbled down the number and dialled.

The phone was picked up on the first ring. "Archie here."

"Archie, Senior Constable Petersen. You have a message for me?"

"Yeah. I've got a pilot, Bob Harrison, in the air who

says he needs to radio-contact you pronto."

"Okay. What's he on?"

"Crack, I'd say. Ha! Sorry, Officer. He's on HF 71."

"Thanks, Archie. You're a gem."

Chapter 37

Bob checked the audio panel switches and adjusted the radio's volume as a hissing noise and air traffic chatter filled the cabin.

"Petersen calling Bravo Kilo Oscar."

He glanced at Butler and grinned. "We've got her. I owe Archie a carton."

"Petersen calling Bravo Kilo Oscar. Come in."

Bob flicked the PTT button for Butler's headset. "I'll let you talk to her, Ric."

"Eileen, it's Ric. Go ahead."

"Ric, good to hear you. Where are you? Wait! Please change to channel 90."

Bob nodded, adjusting the radio frequency.

"Eileen?"

"Receiving."

"We're ten minutes north of Archer River Roadhouse with Wrench in sight. Where are you?"

"Bamaga airstrip. I need a bearing from you, and airspeed."

"I'm handing you over to the pilot, okay?"

"Would that be Professor Harrison?" asked Petersen.

Bob switched off the microphone and raised his eyebrows at Butler. "She's good, Ric," he shouted, "Eileen, eh?" He shook his head knowingly, switching the mic back on.

"Bob Harrison, Officer Petersen. Our heading is 350 degrees, at approximately 112 knots, that's 207 klicks. Do you have instructions?"

"Thanks, Professor Harrison. Can you advise of any changes in course?"

"Roger," said Bob, playfully waggling his head. "What are your plans?"

"Considering our options and refuelling right now. Do you know if the fugitives are armed?"

"Sorry, I don't know. You're in that helicopter, yes? Can you force him to land?"

Petersen glanced at Leech who rolled his eyes sarcastically.

"That is an option we're considering," said Petersen. Leech shook his head. "How's your fuel situation?"

"130 minutes max."

"Which will take you to where?"

"The first airstrip we find in PNG. But Wrench can continue on for at least another forty minutes."

"I see."

"Can you follow them to PNG and arrest them?"

The radio fell quiet.

"No."

Chapter 38

A hush descended over Bob's Cessna. Wrench's plane, an insurmountable few minutes away—or a lifetime—flew above the familiar dark hills of Iron Range. Butler felt certain the fugitives would know they were being followed, but surely they couldn't know a helicopter was en route to intercept them. Since Elder's murder, Stringer had managed to stay one step ahead of the authorities. The more Butler learned of Weagle's dubious past, the more he suspected the monster of leaking information about police operations.

Bob watched him, concern plain on his puckered forehead.

"You okay, Ric? You look miles away."

"I can't help feeling this is going to end badly for someone."

"Yes, hopefully Stringer and Wrench getting arrested."

"I don't know, but I can't let you take more mad risks."

"Sounds like you've been dwelling on that curse business, mate. It's all nonsense."

"Elder might not agree."

"Fair enough. But we have to do whatever we can to get that bird back."

"But where will it stop? There'll be plenty more like Stringer coming to chase the prize."

"Ha! They won't have much luck without that recording," said Jake. "That little bird's a secretive character."

Foreboding shrouded Butler, a sense he couldn't shake. Every click of the aircraft speedometer sealed it deeper into his bones. They were getting in over their heads; chasing a murderer out of the country had to be madness.

Bob interrupted Ric's thoughts. "I've been trying to work out his destination. If he stays on his present course—and he hasn't changed it so far—he's headed to the airstrip at Wipim, in the Trans-Fly."

"Can we make it that far?" said Butler.

"Just. It's a small strip but they usually have fuel there. If Wrench doesn't land there, he will be cutting it close to make the next strip at Takal—especially with this damn headwind."

"But won't Wipim be busy? I thought he'd head somewhere more remote."

"Unless he knows the locals," said Jake.

Bob groaned. "There's a good chance he does. He's been flying to the Western Province for years."

"Surely they wouldn't do us any harm?"

"Ever heard of Michael Rockefeller?" laughed Bob.

"Besides, they don't have to hurt us, just hold us long enough for Wrench to get away."

Jake pushed his head forward between the seats. "Even if we had a rifle?"

"You're starting to sound crazier than Bob," said Butler. "Anyway, we don't have a rifle, do we?"

Jake reached for Thad's coat. He carefully unwrapped the gun and with a sheepish grin on his face passed it to Butler. "I grabbed it from the truck, just in case ... you know."

"Geez, Jake! We've been on the run from the police and all this time you've been carrying a gun!"

"It's not like I would use it," said Jake.

"Then why bring it?" said Butler. He shook his head as Jake retreated into the back seat.

"I'm willing to bet Stringer has a gun," said Bob. "The last thing we want is to start a bloody firefight."

"We're not going to start a fight," said Butler. "That's what the police helicopter is for if it comes to that."

"Hate to put a dampener on things, Ric. But that police helicopter won't enter PNG airspace."

"Why not? He's a murder suspect! And he has a night parrot."

"We have no proof of either, Ric. Even if we did, the police wouldn't go barging into foreign territory uninvited."

Defeat crawled over Butler's skin, like the curse finding its way home. "What the hell do we do then?"

Chapter 39

The EMQ Bell helicopter rose over the lush canopy of the Lockerbie Scrub. The northernmost tip of the Australian mainland quickly came into sight. To the south, Leech had an uninterrupted view of the low heathlands and the direction from which Wrench was fast approaching.

He motioned to Petersen to switch on her headphones. "I'll do what I can, but no promises, okay?"

She nodded gratefully, switching the radio to broadband.

"Police helicopter to Yankee Foxtrot Sierra, Cessna 172. Come in."

She knew Wrench could hear her, but he gave no response.

"Yankee Foxtrot Sierra—Mr. Wrench—please land your aircraft. Your passenger, Dr Col Stringer, alias Dick Orcherton, is wanted for questioning in relation to Jim Elder's murder. Should you not land at the Bamaga airstrip, you will be charged with aiding and abetting."

A single burst of static, then silence.

"Here he comes," said Leech.

A small metallic shape flickered against the blue cloudless sky, its proportions growing with alarming speed. Leech swung the helicopter and faced the plane, accelerating powerfully.

"I'm going to buzz him as hard as I can, try to shake him up."

Petersen braced herself.

"There's Harrison," she said. "Be careful, he's close behind."

Petersen switched to open frequency. "Yankee Foxtrot Sierra, this is your final warning. Land your aircraft now!"

Leech took an aggressive course to the right of the Cessna, but the plane remained doggedly on its course. With a generous margin of safety, Leech swerved to avoid a collision.

"That's as close as I really want to get," said Leech.

"That was close enough for me," nodded Petersen. "He's determined, that's for sure."

Jake lowered the binoculars.

"Bloody hell! Did you see that?"

"Has he changed direction?" asked Bob.

"No, the helicopter buzzed him, pretty close too, but Wrench didn't give an inch."

"What?" Butler reached for the binoculars in time to see the helicopter turn. "Shit! Looks like he's lining up for another go."

The helicopter overtook the Cessna again, this time passing close below and suddenly rocketing up vertically in front. Still the plane held its course.

"Wrench is bloody fearless," said Bob. "I'd be landing in a shot."

The dogfight edged out over the water, the helicopter buzzing the plane twice more with no response.

"The helicopter is blocking his flight path," said Bob. "He's trying to slow him down."

"Bob, don't get any closer," said Butler. "This is getting too real for me."

In a sudden manoeuvre, Wrench's Cessna dipped its port wing and swooped below the helicopter, increasing its speed again.

"He's thumbing his nose at them," said Jake. "He knows they can't follow him across the strait."

"Visibility is worsening," said Bob. "That northerly is bringing some weather our way." He nodded to the north, where a group of rocky islands jutting from whitecaps vanished in a haze. "It will get pretty uncomfortable if we head into that."

Within minutes, the swollen cloud base had forced all three pilots to descend. A dark smear on the horizon marked the New Guinea shoreline. The last two islands of Australian territory hovered defiantly just offshore.

Now less than a minute behind the other two aircraft, Bob saw the helicopter lift dramatically from in front of Wrench's plane. Wrench, with no time to react, shot underneath. Bob backed off quickly. "Damn, that stunt would have scared me. But I think it's too late to do any good now."

The radio crackled to life.

"Petersen calling Bravo Kilo Oscar. Come in."

"I hear you, Eileen."

"I'm sorry, Ric, we have to pull out of this soon."

Butler detected the frustration in her voice.

"We're going after them, Eileen."

"I have to caution you against flying into PNG airspace."

Butler looked at Bob hoping to see a show of strength but saw only trepidation in his friend's eyes.

"Ric. Repeat. Do not go after them. Please."

"You know our position, Eileen. We'll stay in radio contact."

"I can't take this helicopter in after you, Ric."

"Understood, Officer Petersen."

Chapter 40

Butler felt his world disappear in front of him when the helicopter pulled away and swung parallel to New Guinea's shoreline. It seemed it was time to retreat, again. One day there would be a reckoning. God almighty, how many times had he said that to himself? The powerlessness had become loathsome to him. He fixed his eyes on the plane ahead.

"Is he still on track for Wipim?"

"Yeah," replied Bob, "and he's dropping even though we're well below the clouds now. All that slowing and accelerating back there, he's got no chance of making it to Takal."

"And our fuel?"

"Twenty minutes tops."

"How far is Wipim?"

"Ten minutes?"

"If we don't land, can we turn around and make it back to Boigu or Saibai?"

"That's pushing the old girl hard, mate. Boigu,

maybe, but I'd rather put her down here. Anyway, we've got no chance of getting that bird back unless we follow them down."

"It's too risky. We could get shot."

Jake pulled himself forward and stared into Butler's eyes. "We've chased that bastard all the way across the country! We can't give up while there's still a chance."

"I agree, Jake," said Bob. "Besides, we might not make it out of here alive if we don't land. If they're armed, we'll hide in the scrub until they leave. Surely they won't shoot unless they have to."

"We don't know how the locals will react," said Butler.

"It's your call, Ric," said Bob. "But if we're turning around, we should do it now."

"No. We're going to Boigu," said Butler, "And we're taking them with us."

"Ric, you're not making sense, mate. We can't."

"The rifle, Jake. Pass it up."

Bob opened his mouth to speak, but no words came.

"We're going to shoot up the fuel drums in Wipim."

"Struth, Ric. I thought you didn't want a firefight!"

"We can beat them to the fuel drums and I can get a few shots off."

"I don't know," said Bob. "The locals won't be too pleased if we go in all guns blazing."

"That's just it. Wrench won't be so welcome if he brings shit raining down on Wipim. You know how their payback works."

"You really think you can hit some fuel drums?" asked Jake.

"He can, Jake," answered Bob. "He's the best bloody shot you've seen. But Ric, don't you think we're talking about an international incident?"

"We'll worry about that later," said Butler as he reached for the rifle. "Wrench will get the hell out of there if those drums go up. And if he can't make it to Takal, he has no choice but to turn back."

"What's happened to the Ric I used to know?" said Bob.

"Long story, one for the next pool table."

Bob held out his right hand. "All for one."

Butler placed his hand on Bob's and Jake slapped his hand down on top. "One for all."

The thatched roofs of Wipim remained invisible until the plane was almost on top of them. Wrench's flaps flared as he dropped rapidly towards the small straw-coloured landing strip. Abruptly, he withdrew and levelled out.

"What's happening, Jake? Can you see?" asked Butler.

"There're two pigs on the strip. People are running out to chase them off."

"He'll have to approach again."

"Even better," said Butler. "He won't be game to touch down if I've got time to blow that fuel."

"There're the drums," said Jake, "Far end, right-hand corner."

"Out in the open; that's a relief. Okay, Bob, as close as you can," said Butler.

"You're going to have to hit them from about a hundred metres."

"Shit. Can you make it seventy-five?"

"Eighty. We need to stay the hell away from the explosion."

"Jake, watch Wrench. Tell me if he's getting too close," said Bob.

"He's coming around and dropping. I think he's landing in this direction."

"Damn, he's coming in downwind. Are you ready, Ric?"

"I can't get the gun out the window properly. I have to open the door."

"I can't believe we're doing this," said Bob.

Butler looked steadily back at him. "It's our best chance, Bob. I'm taking it."

Bob saw an unfamiliar resolve in his friend's eyes. "Righto. I'm going in as low as I dare, but those drums will go by really fast."

Butler nodded, looking to the ground and bracing the rifle against his shoulder. Bob nervously rubbed his knuckles against his shirt before levelling out on the final approach.

"He's pulling up, he's seen us," said Jake.

The moment the drums came into sight, Butler fired four rounds in quick succession, pulling the gun up over the door, and shooting twice more at the receding target.

"Shit! I've missed!"

Bob pulled up on the stick and sped up. "One more pass, Ric. Wrench is going around again."

Butler scrambled to reload.

"Wrench is behind us!" yelled Jake.

Bob turned dangerously close to the treetops, passing through a scattering of startled lorikeets before he straightened for the second pass, this time over the low scrub to the side of the strip.

"Wrench is straightening up too," said Jake.

"Line me up, Bob," said Butler. He held the rifle up, flipped off his headphones, and closed his eyes. Filling his lungs, his mind brimmed with the bird, the spinifex, the old man, and his mother. He felt the plane level out and slow. Opening his eyes, he searched out the fuel drums and pressed his left eye to the sight. The drums found the crosshairs; he breathed out and fired.

The air filled with fire and a loud roar pushed the plane onto its side. The door slammed closed above him. Beneath him Bob was white-faced, but his hands automatically fought to right the plane. Butler glanced over his shoulder and met Jake's horrified face staring back at him.

"Jake!" yelled Butler. "Where's the other plane?"

Jake blinked a few times then lifted the binoculars to his head. "It worked! He's turning away from the strip."

"It worked! He's running!" said Bob.

A wild "Whoop" filled the cockpit.

Chapter 41

Butler spoke into his headset. "Bravo Kilo Oscar to Petersen."

"Ric? Was that an explosion?"

"The fuel drums at Wipim went up in smoke. Wrench has turned back and is heading south."

"What happened?"

"I'll fill you in later. We have to get back to Boigu before our fuel runs out."

Bob swung the plane, easing back on the throttle, and staying low. Butler reached over and grabbed his shoulder. "We did it!"

"It's not over yet, Ric. We're running on fumes, mate."

"You said we had twenty minutes."

"That was in level flight, mate."

Butler turned to see Jake still looked dazed. "Jake, are you hurt?"

Jake shook his head slowly, breathing in for what seemed the first time in minutes. "I'm okay. A bit green maybe."

Bob scoured the horizon. Boigu should have been in sight, but a thick haze descended across the wild sea. Wind buffeted them from behind and a spattering of raindrops hit the windscreen. "That's all we bloody need," muttered Bob. "There will be a plane and a helicopter on the runway, and we won't be able to see what's going on."

Butler's mind raced. "We've almost got him; surely Stringer will go quietly now?"

"That's the least of our problems, mate!" said Bob. "This is my worst bloody nightmare, having to ditch her in the sea."

"We'll make it, Bob. We have to."

The full force of the downpour pounded against the windshield as Bob lined the plane up to land. Buffeting wind threw the Cessna into a seesawing action that brought a string of profanities from him.

Butler squinted to see through the sheets of rain driving towards them. "There! Mangroves."

Bob dropped abruptly, passing over the rubbish tip at the end of the runway. "Thanks be to——"

"Holy Shit!" yelled Butler. "Pull up! Pull up!"

Bob swore between clenched teeth as he pulled up with all his strength. In the second before they rose back into the clouds, he saw Wrench's plane parked across the middle of the strip.

"Someone's running away from the plane," yelled Butler. "They're headed towards the beach."

"Jake, what's happening on the strip?" said Bob.

"There's people running towards the plane. Maybe they're trying to move it."

Bob swung out over the grey, roiling water. As he turned to line up for the runway, the plane lurched as the prop missed a beat. "I bloody hope so," said Bob. "Otherwise, we're going to ditch. Hang on!"

Butler couldn't grip his seat any tighter. He was looking over his shoulder for Jake, but the violence of Bob's turn threw him off balance. Whitecaps whipped past the wingtip as Bob pulled level to face the storm. The engine sputtered and fell silent. All they could hear was the howling weather and their own panicked breath.

Chapter 42

"Brace yourselves! We're going in."

"We're done for!" said Jake. "If the crash doesn't kill us, the crocs will."

"Hang on," yelled Bob.

Butler looked in panic at the fast-approaching waves just as a dugout canoe motored from the shore into the heavy swell. No islander would go out in this! He squinted until the boatman—bearded, with a backpack—became visible. He was waving a gun towards the shore.

"It's him!" yelled Butler, just as the raging sea smashed into the plane's undercarriage with a shattering roar.

The seatback slammed into Butler throwing him forwards into the windshield, his seatbelt cutting deeply into his flesh. The plane skidded across the water, each wave slamming it upwards until its momentum abruptly ceased and its heavy nose pulled them down.

"Out! Get out, quick!" yelled Bob.

Butler turned to see Jake lying immobile on the back seat. Blood oozed from his forehead. Grabbing at his own harness, he felt a stabbing pain in his side. As he leaned into the back seat to grab Jake, fire exploded in his ribs.

"Ric! Get out. I'll pass him down," yelled Bob.

Butler opened his door and fell into the salty murk. He rose above the waves and saw the empty canoe rocking violently in their bow wave, only fifty metres away. "The bird. Where is it?"

"Ric!"

He twisted back to the plane to see Jake's body falling feet first. Jake squirmed in his arms, his weight pushing Butler under the waves. He kicked as hard as he could, the salty wind whipping his face.

"I'll take him," yelled Bob. "It's not far."

"The canoe!" said Butler.

"Don't be a bloody id——" yelled Bob.

Bob's warning disappeared into the wind as Butler swam away. Each stroke tortured his ribs, his gasps sucking in saltwater. He was halfway to the canoe when a burly shape clambered into it. He stroked harder, willing himself to ignore the pain. Stringer hauled on the outboard. His mouth dropped open when he saw Butler bear down on him.

"You don't bloody give up, do you," he yelled, as he reached into his coat and pulled a gun out. "Piss off!" He aimed the gun at Butler's head and fired.

Chapter 43

The sound of gunshots filled the air as Bob landed ashore with an unconscious Jake. Petersen and Leech sprinted towards him.

"Where's Ric?" yelled Petersen.

"He's gone after Stringer," said Bob as he collapsed onto the ground.

"Ray!" yelled Petersen. "Get the bloody chopper!"

Leech held onto his cap in the roaring wind but had the good sense not to argue. He ran towards the chopper.

Butler had nowhere to go but underwater. He dived, kicking as hard as he could under the canoe's hull and up the other side. When he grabbed the canoe's gunwale, Stringer cursed and threw the gun at him, striking him hard on the right cheekbone. Butler flinched as Stringer pulled once more on the outboard's pull rope. The engine spat, stuttered, and fired. He flicked his finger at Butler.

Butler saw the canoe, the bird, and his mother's

face slipping away from him. Sod this! A roar thundered from the centre of his chest, spurring him into one last desperate effort. He reached out for the prow of the boat just as Stringer revved the throttle. The sudden shift in weight caused the engine to buck and stall.

"I've had enough of you!" yelled Stringer, raising a paddle over his head.

Butler recoiled at the shark-like deadness in Stringer's eyes but refused to let go of the boat. He squeezed his eyes shut waiting for the blow, but as the paddle reached the height of its arc, the canoe collided with a solid object under the water. The boat rocked violently, throwing Stringer backwards into the water. Butler's legs brushed against something that flexed as it passed. He frantically hauled himself into the canoe.

Within arm's reach of the canoe, Stringer rose to the surface. His face was filled with panic. Butler reached towards his flailing hands but the bearded face was pulled underwater. He surfaced again, tried to cry out, but disappeared as if weighted down. The swirl of a great scaled tail broke the surface, and Butler stumbled backwards, falling heavily into the bottom of the canoe.

Reeling with shock, he slumped against the rough wood bench and panted heavily. Seawater pushed up through his throat and he retched until his eyes felt as if they'd pop out. Then, under the bench and miraculously still looped around an oar, he spotted a backpack.

He straddled the seat and lifted the pack into his lap, his heart pounding. Inside, a small, solid cardboard box was sodden. Fear and panic overwhelmed him. Was there any chance? Gently he lifted the lid, gasping when he sighted the emerald shape hunched motionless in a corner. His hand shook as he reached for it. He felt only coldness.

He stroked the inert body, feeling its spine through the feathers. His eyes stung for the bird, as he touched its small skull, chest, and tail feathers.

He yelled into the wind. "Nooooo――!"

Then his finger stung as the frightened bird bit down on it savagely.

"Ouch!" cried Butler, overcome with joy and urgency. Before the bird could take off a fingernail, he grasped it in both hands, its black eyes defiantly boring into his face. He leaned closer and its sharp beak reached for his nose. "You're a tough little nut!" he said.

In the dying light, the swell rolled higher, the canoe rapidly drifting away from the settlement.

"Sorry, bird," he muttered as he placed it back in the box and zipped up the pack.

He stood and yanked hard on the motor. Nothing. Five more pulls and still no sound. With one last exhausted pull he heaved with everything he had. The air erupted with a roar, but the motor remained still and cold. "How the ..."

Butler was bathed in a light whiter than day as the helicopter hovered overhead. He stood and waved which caused the canoe to lurch wildly. He crouched in the hull, the storm buffeting him with a renewed malevolence. A figure descended on a winch line; wild blonde hair haloed against the floodlight.

"Ric!" called Petersen. She swung erratically, dropping rapidly towards the canoe. He reached for her outstretched hand, pulling her into the boat. Her grey eyes stared breathlessly, until the next wave hit.

"Quick! Get this on!" she yelled, handing him a harness.

"Wait, take this first," he shouted, lifting the backpack.

"Come on, Ric, we have to get out of here. Hold on."

He slipped the harness on. Petersen buckled him to her with one hand and waved to the helicopter with the other. Butler clung to the backpack.

"Stringer?" she yelled, as they collapsed onto the helicopter's floor.

He shook his head. The revving of the rotors made speaking impossible.

Chapter 44

Butler peeped into the recovery room where Jake had been taken after his examination. Bamaga Hospital was well appointed, which gave him confidence his friend was in good hands. He walked back along the corridor to where Petersen sat.

"How are your ribs?" she asked.

"Nothing a good sleep won't fix."

She lowered her voice so those passing couldn't hear. "Do you think Stringer drowned?"

"No. I think he got taken by a croc. There was something big in the water that scared the shit out of me, enough so I didn't jump in after him."

"If it was a croc, he was unlucky. The locals hunt everything on those islands."

Sitting in the sparse but functional corridor, Butler felt strangely reluctant to call Petersen by her first name now that she sat face-to-face with him. He noticed her aloof, polished persona had given way to a softer presence and she appeared more comfortable in a pair of cargo pants and trekking boots than in her office uniform.

Her cheeks reddened under Butler's stare.

To break the tension, he asked, "What's going to happen to Wrench?"

"He's in Boigu lock-up but co-operating. He denied all knowledge of Elder's murder and claimed the only reason he flew on after Bamaga was because Stringer pulled a gun on him. And ..." Petersen hesitated.

"Yes, what else?"

"Strictly between you and me, he was pressured by a third party."

"Weagle! You don't have to tell me. I knew that bastard was crooked." Petersen's poker face confirmed he was right.

"Your boss has a finger in a lot of pies," she said.

"Not for long, I hope."

He sat back in his chair and caressed the new cardboard box on his lap.

"Will there be any charges against me?"

"No. The night parrot recording was in Stringer's backpack. It will be used in evidence, as will the bird."

Butler clutched the box protectively.

"The bird?"

"Yes. Its identity will need to be verified independently. Don't worry, it will be cared for carefully."

"By who?"

"An expert aviculturist, I imagine. Working from within our evidence system."

"And then?"

"I don't know, Ric."

"But I'm looking after it tonight, right?"

"Yes," she smiled. "You seem attached to it."

Butler laughed. "I was until he showed me upfront who was boss." He held up his swollen finger.

Petersen examined it carefully, taking his hand in hers. "You should get that taken care of," she said, meeting his eyes softly. For a fleeting moment, they felt each other's awkwardness. She regained her composure by standing up.

"I should get some sleep. I hope these hospital beds are comfortable, although I won't need any rocking. See you in the morning, Ric." She turned to leave.

"Eileen?"

"Yes?" She turned, expectantly.

"These might be useful." He handed her a small clump of feathers. "For evidence; DNA analysis."

She stared at his offering uncertainly.

"Ah, okay. Thanks. Goodnight."

"Goodnight, Eileen."

Chapter 45

Shortly after daybreak, Jake woke up and squinted towards the window.

"Oi," Bob whispered.

"Bob," said Jake, a little hoarsely.

"How are you feeling, mate?"

"Sore, but not too bad, considering."

"You had a good sleep."

"Yeah, and some strange dreams. Ric was driving along some endless dirt road. And I was plummeting towards the earth."

"Mmm. Well, they reckon you haven't done any lasting damage."

"Great! But I won't be getting in a plane again anytime soon. No offence," he chuckled.

"None taken. Sorry touchdown was a bit rough."

"Ric's catching up on some sleep, eh?"

Bob smiled sheepishly. "Ehm, maybe."

"What do you mean?"

"He's gone, mate, took off before dawn."

"What? Where to?"

"He said you'll know."

Jake's frown grew into a wide-eyed grin.

"The bugger! Where did he get a car?"

"That's what I said. He just gave me that look and said, 'Don't ask.'"

Just then Petersen opened the door and looked in. She glanced around the room. "Ric's still sleeping, then?"

"He'll turn up," they said.

Jake winced as he belly-laughed.

"Allan zee, Ric. Allan zee!"

Acknowledgements

Many thanks to Donna Mulvenna and Margi Prideaux at Stormbird Press for welcoming me to their publishing house as if to a family, for sticking with my fledgling book through the process of moulding it into publishable form, and for inviting me to illustrate the cover. To Donna in particular, thank you for your unlimited patience and persistence in helping to bash my manuscript into its very best self. On top of the usual demands of publishing, Stormbird endured the direct impacts of the horrendous bushfire season of 2020 and the all-pervading effects of the coronavirus pandemic, yet remained committed to their mission; we are all enriched by their dedication.

Special thanks to Rob Heinsohn and Tani Cooper, who generously gave their time to provide focused criticism of earlier drafts of my manuscript and ongoing encouragement throughout the long gestation of this book. My old friend Chris Harriss also gave valuable advice for which I am very grateful.

I am eternally grateful to my family for their support and love and for providing an environment where reading and writing are valued.

About John Grant

John Grant grew up in Ireland where his love of the outdoors and especially wildlife was nurtured by parents and teachers. A desire to find work doing what he loved led him to study for a degree in zoology at University College Dublin, culminating in an honour's thesis on the foraging ecology of shorebirds. His research work continued with a PhD scholarship to the Australian National University in Canberra, where he studied the foraging behaviour of insectivorous bats. After several long, dark years with bats, he moved to North Queensland in 1987 and began a lasting love affair with the soon-to-be World Heritage rainforests of the Wet Tropics. Here he started long-term studies of rainforest bird communities and the Sarus Cranes which overwinter on the Atherton Tablelands and breed on the Gulf of Carpentaria wetlands. After some years as a wildlife guide in the tourism industry and some work as a consultant ecologist in the Wet Tropics and Cape York areas, his teaching career began in earnest when he moved to the Centre for Rainforest Studies near Yungaburra. He taught forest ecology and conservation courses there for several years before moving to Cairns as director of the Natural and Cultural Ecology program of the School for International Training. After six years directing this program, he stepped back to his current part-time teaching role and also developed a new program on biodiversity and conservation, which he now teaches annually in Indonesia.

John has been an active member of several community-based conservation organisations, especially those associated with reforestation, and has been a team leader for Australian Conservation Volunteers. He is past president and vice-president of the Tree Kangaroo and Mammal Group, based on the Atherton Tablelands, where he has lived for many years.

His other interests include art, especially wildlife art, which he practices in a variety of media, most often pencil, watercolour and acrylic. He has held two solo exhibitions of his work. Photography, bushwalking and reading are more of his favourite activities.

Are you a changemaker?

Stories about our world, and our relationship with nature, have been communicated among wise souls and changemakers for countless generations.

People willing to courageously make a difference in the world have gathered around campfires and sat under the limbs of mighty trees to be nurtured by this wisdom. Story is how humanity has always shared moral tales, empowered itself with knowledge, and paid hope forward into the future.

Our authors embody this spirit. They write with reverence, wisdom, and inspiration about the places, plants and animals, habitats and ecosystems, of our shared home—*Earth*.

In our new online place—*The Gathering*—you can connect directly with our brave authors and other bold thinkers to unshackle creative action. We all hold the power to make positive change. We just need a safe space to soar like feathers in the wind.

To connect with brave authors, like John Grant, join *The Gathering* now.

www.stormbirdpress.com

Stormbird Press is a proud signatory to the *United Nations SDG Publishers Compact*. At the time of publishing this title, our focus in on contributions to *SDG 13: Climate Action, SDG 14: Life Below Water, SDG 15: Life on Land, and SDG 16: Peace, Justice* and *Strong Institutions*.

www.ingramcontent.com/pod-product-compliance
Lightning Source LLC
Chambersburg PA
CBHW020400030726
47496CB00007B/2231